FELIX HOFFMANN

HANS IN LUCK

SEVEN STORIES
BY THE BROTHERS GRIMM

North
South

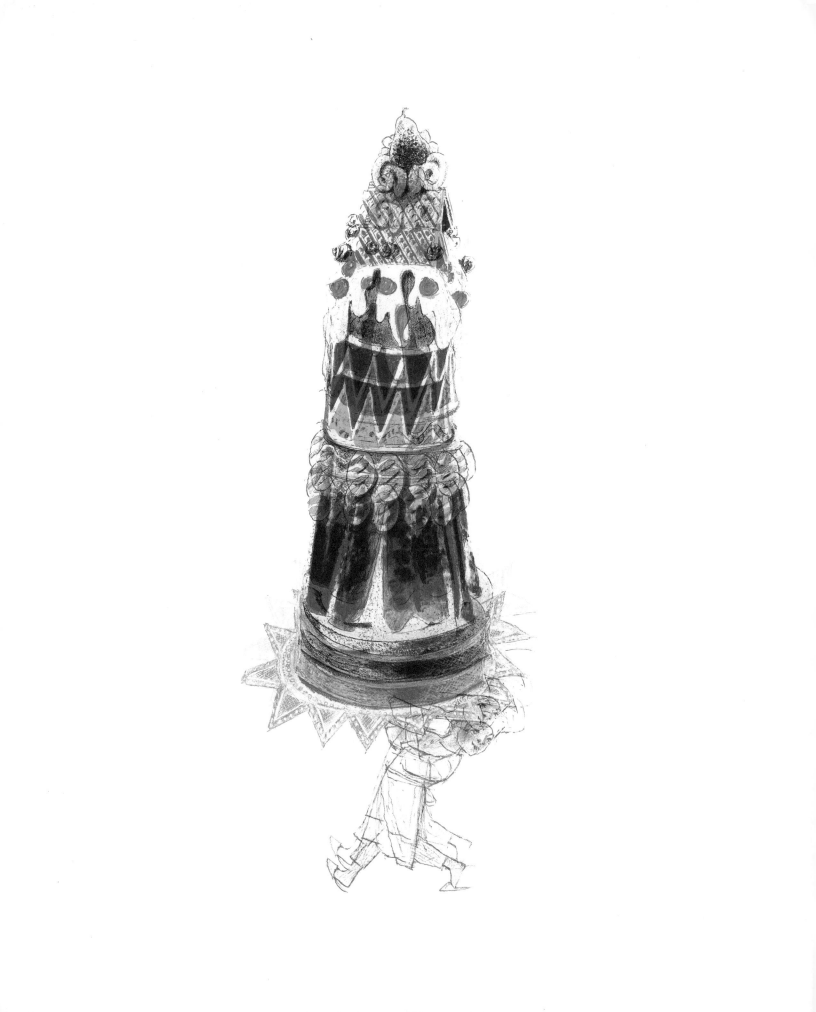

RAPUNZEL

Retold by Felix Hoffmann

There were once a husband and wife who for a long time had wished they could have a child. They had a house with a little garden and would often sit there in the evenings on the patio and watch as night fell. They would also look out into the neighbor's large garden, which was full of the loveliest flowers and herbs. Nobody dared to enter there, because it belonged to a sorceress who had great powers and was feared by everyone.

One evening, when they were sitting there again, the woman caught sight of a vegetable patch that was planted with beautiful lamb's lettuces, and they looked so fresh and green that she had a great desire to eat some of them. The desire became stronger day by day, and as she knew that she could not have any, she became very thin, and looked pale and miserable. Her husband was alarmed and asked, "What is wrong with you, dear wife?" "Alas!" she answered, "if I do not get to eat any of the lamb's lettuces from the garden next to our house, I shall die." And so the man, who loved her, thought, "Rather than let your wife die, you should go and get her some of the lamb's lettuces, no matter what the consequences might be." And so at dusk he climbed over the wall into the sorceress's garden, hurriedly plucked a handful of lettuces, and took them to his wife. She immediately made a salad out of them, and hungrily gobbled it up.

The lettuces, however, had tasted so good that the next day her desire for them was three times greater than before. If she were to have any rest, her husband would have to climb back into the garden again. And so he returned there at dusk. But this time when he was standing in the strange garden he received a terrible shock, because from behind the tall tree stepped the sorceress! "How dare you climb into my garden," she cried, her face twisted with rage, "and like a thief steal my lamb's lettuces from me. You will suffer for this!" "Oh," he answered, "please let mercy outweigh justice, because I only resolved to do this out of dire need. My wife saw your lamb's lettuces from a distance, and she has such a deep yearning for them that she will die if she doesn't have some of them to eat." Then the sorceress calmed down and said to him, "If things are as you say they are, then I shall allow you to take as many of the lamb's lettuces as you like. But if you come here again, you must give me the child that your wife is going to bring into the world. It will be happy here with me, and I shall look after it like a mother." The man hurried away, determined never to return.

13

But after a few days, the man's wife pleaded fervently that he should go and get some lamb's lettuces just once more, and so he waited till dark and crept through the garden. What a shock he had when again the sorceress was suddenly standing right behind him! She reminded him of his promise, and had no pity on him.

When the baby was born, the sorceress appeared, named the child Rapunzel, and immediately took her away.

When the sorceress wanted to go in, she stood down below and called out:

> "Rapunzel, Rapunzel,
> Let down your hair for me!"

Rapunzel had wonderful long hair, as fine as spun gold. When she heard the voice of the sorceress, she untied her braids, and wrapped them round a hook on the window. From there her hair reached down twenty cubits, and the sorceress climbed up.

A few years later, it happened that the king's son came riding through the forest and came upon the tower. He heard someone singing, and the sound was so sweet that he stopped and listened. It was Rapunzel, who in her solitude passed the time by exercising her sweet voice. The king's son wanted to climb up to her and he looked for a door into the tower, but there was none to be seen.

He rode home. But the song had touched his heart so deeply that every day he rode out into the forest and listened. One day, when he was standing behind a tree, he saw the sorceress arrive and heard her call out:

> "Rapunzel, Rapunzel,
> Let down your hair for me!"

Then Rapunzel let down her braids, and the sorceress climbed up to her. The king's son thought, "If that's the ladder one climbs up, then I'll try my luck as well."

The following day, when it started to get dark, he went to the tower and called out:

> "Rapunzel, Rapunzel,
> Let down your hair for me!"

The hair came down immediately, and the king's son climbed up it. At first Rapunzel was terrified when a man appeared before her, because she had never seen a man before. But the king's son began to talk to her in a very friendly way, and he told her that his heart had been so touched by her singing that he had been unable to get any rest and simply had to see her. Then Rapunzel was no longer afraid, and when he asked her if she would marry him, and she could see how young and handsome he was, she thought, "He will love me more than old Mother Gothel," and so she said yes and put her hand in his. She said, "I will gladly go with you, but I don't know how I can get down. Each time you come, bring a skein of silk with you, and I will weave a ladder out of it, so when it is ready I'll climb down and you can take me with you on your horse." They agreed that until then he should come to her every evening, because the old woman came during the day.

The sorceress did not notice anything until one day Rapunzel said to her, "Mother Gothel, tell me, why is it that you are much heavier for me to pull up than the young son of the king, who reaches me in just a moment."

"Oh, you wicked child!" cried the sorceress. "What is this I hear you say? I thought I had kept you away from the whole world, but you have deceived me!" In her anger, she seized hold of Rapunzel's beautiful tresses, wrapped them round her left hand a few times, grasped a pair of scissors with her right hand, and snippety-snip, she cut them all off, and the lovely braids lay on the floor.

The king's son came in the evening and called out:

> "Rapunzel, Rapunzel,
> Let down your hair for me!"

The wicked woman hung Rapunzel's hair out of the window, and the king's son climbed up as before. But when he had almost reached the top, the old woman looked out and hissed, "Aha, you want to come and get your true love, but the beautiful bird is no longer in the nest and she will sing no more because the cat has eaten her, and it will also scratch your eyes out!" So saying, she cut the braids right through, and the king's son fell down into the depths, where thorns stabbed him in the eyes.

Rapunzel, whose heart almost broke when she saw and heard all this, immediately leapt after him, but she was not injured at all. She looked for her loved one, and when she found him, she took him in her arms and wept bitter tears. The teardrops fell into his eyes, and they became clear again, and he could see just as he had seen before.

He took Rapunzel with him to his kingdom, where she became his queen, and they lived happily ever after.

The wicked sorceress, however, could no longer get out of the tower, which had no stairs and no doors. She became smaller and smaller until she looked like a tiny shriveled apple. Then a big bird picked her up and took her back to the nest for its chicks to eat. And wasn't that what she deserved?

THE WOLF
AND THE SEVEN
LITTLE KIDS

Once upon a time there was an old mother goat who had seven little kids, and she loved them just as all mothers love their children.

One day she was going out to look for food, so she called all her seven little kids and told them, "Dear children, I'm going into the wood, so mind you watch for the wolf! If he gets in here, he'll eat you up. The wicked creature often disguises himself, but you can recognize him easily by his hoarse voice and his black feet."

"We promise to be careful, dear mother," said the seven little kids. "Don't worry!"

So Old Mother Goat bleated good-bye and went on her way.

Before long there was a knock at the door, and the seven little kids heard someone say, "Open the door, dear children! Here's your mother back with something for each of you." But the seven little kids wouldn't open the door. "You're not our mother!" they called back. "Our mother has a soft, gentle voice, but yours is hoarse. You're the wolf!"

So the wolf went to the village store and bought a big piece of chalk.
He ate it, and it made his voice soft and gentle.
He came back and knocked on the door again. "Open the door, dear children!
Here's your mother back with something for each of you."
But one of the wolf's black feet was showing at the window; and when
the seven little kids saw it, they said, "We won't open the door! Our mother's
feet are all white, and yours aren't. You're the wolf!"

The wolf went to the baker and said, "I've hurt my paw! Please put some dough on it!" And when the baker had covered his paw with dough, the wolf went off to the miller and said, "Sprinkle some white flour on my paw."

The miller thought, "This wolf is planning to trick someone!" and refused.

But the wolf said, "If you don't do as I say, I'll eat you up!" The miller was afraid and sprinkled white flour on the wolf's paw.

Then the wicked wolf went back to the house for the third time, knocked on the door, and said, "Open the door, children! Your dear mother is home from the wood with something for each of you."

"Show us your feet first!" said the seven little kids. "Then we'll know whether you're our dear mother or not."

So the wolf held up his white paws to the window,
and when the seven little kids saw them, they opened the door.

But it was the wolf who came in! The seven little kids were scared and tried to hide. One hid under the table, the second in the dresser, the third on the stove, the fourth under the bench, the fifth in the corner, the sixth under the stove, and the seventh inside the grandfather clock.

But the wolf found them and gobbled up every single one of them, except the youngest, who was hiding inside the grandfather clock. The wolf didn't find him.

When the wolf had eaten the six little kids, he strolled out of the house, lay down in the meadow under a tree, and went to sleep.

A little later, Old Mother Goat came home. Oh, what a sight met her eyes! The door of the house was wide-open; the table, chairs, and benches had been knocked over; the milk jug was broken; the curtain was torn. She looked for her children, but they were nowhere to be found. She called their names, one by one, but there was no answer.

At last, when she called the youngest, a tiny voice replied,
"Here I am, dear mother, hiding in the grandfather clock."
She helped him out, and he told her the wolf had come to eat all the others.
Oh, how Old Mother Goat wept for her six little kids!

Then, in her sorrow, Old Mother Goat went out of the house
with the youngest little kid in her arms.

When she came to the meadow, she found the wolf sound asleep under a tree, and she saw something moving inside his full stomach. "My goodness," she thought. "Can my poor children still be alive in there?"

Old Mother Goat ran home for scissors, a needle, and thread. Then she began cutting open the wicked wolf's stomach. No sooner had she made the first cut than one of the little kids put its head out, and as she went on cutting, all six jumped out one by one. They were all alive and had come to no harm, because in his greed, the wicked wolf had swallowed them whole.

How happy they were! They hugged their dear mother and hopped about merrily.

But Old Mother Goat said, "Go and find some big rocks in the stream, and we'll fill the wicked wolf's stomach with them while he lies there asleep."

So the seven little kids hurried off to collect rocks and put
as many as they could in the wolf's stomach.

Then Old Mother Goat quickly sewed it up again.

When the wolf finally woke up, he was thirsty, so he decided to go to the well for a drink. But as he began to move about, the rocks in his stomach rattled and clattered.

"What's that thumping and bumping inside me?" cried the wolf. "I ate six little kids, but it feels like rocks."

And when the wolf came to the well and leaned over to drink,
the heavy rocks dragged him in and he was drowned.

When the seven little kids saw the wolf
disappear, they ran up, shouting,

> "The wolf is dead!
> The wolf is dead!"

and Old Mother Goat and her seven little kids
danced around the well for joy.

SLEEPING BEAUTY

There once lived a king and queen who longed to have children. One day, when the queen was bathing in the river, a frog jumped out onto the bank beside her. "Your dearest wish will be granted," he said. "Within a year you will have a daughter."

The frog's promise came true, and the queen had a beautiful baby girl. The king was so delighted he decided to give a great feast to celebrate the birth.

The king invited not only his relatives, friends, and acquaintances, but also the wise women of the kingdom, hoping this would make them kind and friendly toward his child. There were thirteen wise women, but he had only twelve golden plates, so one of them wouldn't be invited.

It was a wonderful feast! When it was over, the wise women gathered around the cradle to give their magical gifts to the child. One gave virtue, another beauty, another wealth, and so they continued, until the child had everything she could have wished for.

When eleven of the wise women had given their gifts, the thirteenth
suddenly appeared, furious that she had not been invited. Without a
word or a glance at anyone, she strode into the room and cried in a shrill voice:
"When the king's daughter is fifteen years old, she will prick her finger on a
spindle and fall down dead!" Then she vanished.

For a moment everyone stood in shocked silence, but then the twelfth wise
woman stepped forward. "I still have a wish to grant," she said. "I cannot
lift the curse, only soften it. The king's daughter will not die, but fall asleep
for a hundred years."

Hoping to protect his dear child from this dreadful fate, the king ordered that every spindle in the kingdom be burned.

As the princess grew, she was as good and kind and beautiful as the wise women had promised. All who met her loved her.

On the morning of her
fifteenth birthday, the
king and queen went out,
and the princess was
left alone. She decided
to explore the castle
and wandered around
peering into any rooms
that looked interesting.
After some time she
came to an old tower.

She climbed its narrow, winding staircase and found a little door. In the lock was a rusty key. When she turned it, the door sprang open. In the little room sat an old woman busily spinning flax.

"Good morning," said the princess. "What are you doing?"

"I'm spinning," said the old woman.

"What is that thing, bobbing about so prettily?" asked the princess, reaching for the spindle. No sooner had she touched it than she pricked her finger, and the wise woman's curse began to work.

She fell into a deep sleep, and sleep took hold of the whole castle—the king and queen, who had just entered the Great Hall, fell asleep, and so did all their court.

Then the horses in the stable fell asleep, the dogs in the yard, the doves on the roof, and the flies on the wall. Even the fire in the hearth flickered and died down; the roast stopped sizzling; and the cook, who was about to box the kitchen boy's ear, let him go and fell asleep, too.

Even the wind settled down to sleep, and all around the castle not a leaf stirred. A hedge of briars began to grow around the castle walls. Year by year it grew higher and higher until the whole castle—even the flags on the top of its towers—was hidden.

The story of the beautiful sleeping Princess Briar Rose (for that was her name) spread far and wide. Princes heard it and came to cut their way through the briars. But they could not do it. The thorns clung together as if they had hands, and the poor young men were trapped.

Many, many years later, another prince came to the kingdom and heard the story of the thorn hedge. An old man told him there was supposed to be a castle behind it, in which a beautiful princess named Briar Rose had been sleeping for a hundred years—and the king and queen and all the court with her.

The old man had heard from his grandfather that many princes had tried to get through the hedge, but they had all been caught in the thorns and died.

The prince said, "I'm not afraid. I will go and find the beautiful Briar Rose."
He would not listen to the old man's warnings.

But a hundred years had now passed, and the day had come for Briar Rose
to wake up. As the prince walked toward the thorn hedge, the briars burst into
flower and parted of their own accord to let him through.

In the castle courtyard, he saw the horses and the hunting dogs lying fast asleep and the doves perching on the roof with their heads tucked under their wings.

Inside, the flies were asleep on the walls, the cook still had his hand raised to hit the boy, and the kitchen maid sat holding the black hen that she had started to pluck.

The prince came to the Great Hall and saw the whole court lying on the floor, and the king and queen sleeping on their thrones. Everything was so quiet he could hear himself breathing. On he went, and at last he came to the old tower and opened the door of the little room where Briar Rose lay asleep.

She looked so beautiful that he bent down and kissed her. As soon as she felt the touch, Briar Rose woke up and looked lovingly at the prince.

As the prince and princess went down the stairs together, the king and queen and all the court woke up and looked at each other wide-eyed. The horses in the yard stood up and shook themselves; the hunting dogs leaped up and wagged their tails; the doves on the roof looked around and flew into the field; the flies crept up the wall; the fire in the kitchen flared up and cooked the food; the roast sizzled again; the cook boxed the kitchen boy on the ear and made him yelp; and the maid finished plucking the chicken.

Soon afterward, the prince and Briar Rose were married and lived happily ever after.

THE SEVEN
RAVENS

There was once a man who had seven sons, and last of all one daughter.

Although the little girl was very pretty, she was so weak and small that they thought she could not live; but they said she should at once be christened.

So the father sent one of his sons in haste to the spring to get some water, but the other six ran with him. Each wanted to be first at drawing the water, and so they were in such a hurry that all let their pitchers fall into the well, and they stood very foolishly looking at one another, and did not know what to do, for none dared go home.

In the meantime the father was uneasy, and could not tell what made the young men stay so long. "Surely," said he, "the whole seven must have forgotten themselves over some game of play"; and when he had waited still longer and yet they did not come, he flew into a rage and wished them all turned into ravens. Scarcely had he spoken these words when he heard a croaking over his head, and looked up and saw seven ravens as black as coal flying round and round.

Sorry as he was to see his wish so fulfilled, he did not know how what was done could be undone, and comforted himself as well as he could for the loss of his seven sons with his dear little daughter, who soon became stronger and every day more beautiful.

For a long time she did not know that she had ever had any brothers; for her father and mother took care not to speak of them before her: but one day by chance she heard the people about her speak of them. "Yes," said they, "she is beautiful indeed, but still 'tis a pity that her brothers should have been lost for her sake." Then she was much grieved, and went to her father and mother, and asked if she had any brothers, and what had become of them. So they dared no longer hide the truth from her, but said it was the will of Heaven, and that her birth was only the innocent cause of it.

But the little girl mourned sadly about it every day, and thought herself bound to do all she could to bring her brothers back.

And she had neither rest nor ease, till at length one day she stole away, and set out into the wide world to find her brothers, wherever they might be, and free them, whatever it might cost her.

She took nothing with her but a little ring that her father and mother had given her, a loaf of bread in case she should be hungry, a little pitcher of water in case she should be thirsty, and a little stool to rest upon when she should be weary.

Thus she went on and on, and journeyed till she came to the world's end.

Then she came to the sun, but the sun looked much too hot and fiery.

So she ran away quickly to the moon, but the moon was cold and chilly, and said, "I smell flesh and blood this way!"

So she took herself away in a hurry and came to the stars, and they were friendly and kind to her, and each star sat upon its own little stool; but the morning star rose up and gave her a little piece of wood, and said, "If you have not this little piece of wood, you cannot unlock the castle that stands on the glass-mountain, and there your brothers live."

The little girl took the piece of wood, rolled it up in a little cloth, and went on again until she came to the glass-mountain, and found the door shut. Then she felt for the little piece of wood; but when she unwrapped the cloth it was not there, and she saw she had lost the gift of the good stars. What was to be done? She wanted to save her brothers, and had no key to the castle of the glass-mountain; so this faithful little sister took a knife out of her pocket and cut off her little finger, which was just the size of the piece of wood she had lost, and put it in the door and opened it.

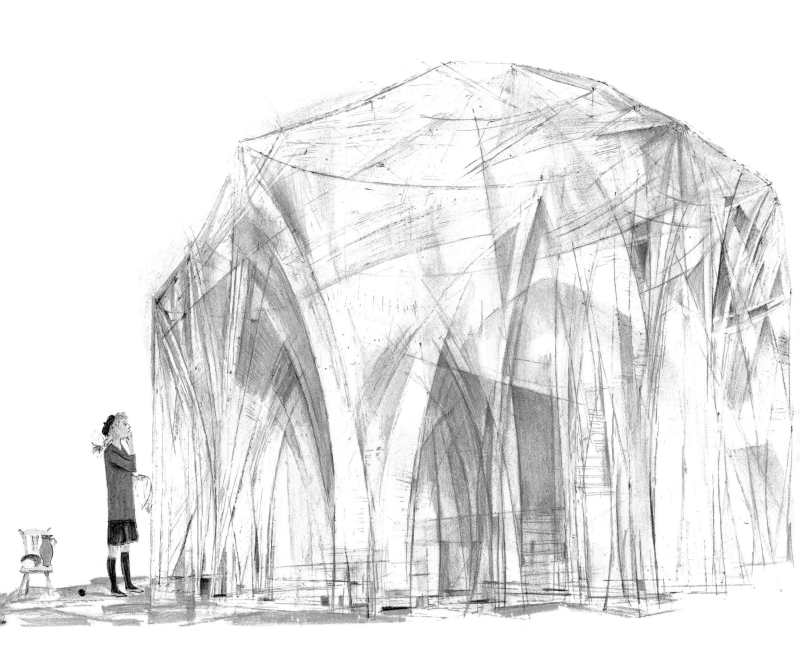

As she went in, a dwarf came up to her, and said, "What are you seeking?" "I seek for my brothers, the seven ravens," she answered. Then the dwarf said, "My masters are not at home; but if you will wait till they come, pray step in."

Now the dwarf was getting their dinner ready, and he brought their food upon seven little plates, and their drink in seven little glasses, and set them upon the table, and out of each little plate their sister ate a small piece, and out of each little glass she drank a small drop; but she let the ring that she had brought with her fall into the last glass. All of a sudden she heard a fluttering and croaking in the air, and the dwarf said, "Here come my masters."

When they came in, they wanted to eat and drink, and looked for their little plates and glasses. Then said one after the other, "Who has eaten from my little plate? And who has been drinking out of my little glass?"

"Caw! Caw! well I ween Mortal lips have this way been."

When the seventh came to the bottom of his glass, and found there the ring, he looked at it, and knew that it was his father's and mother's, and said, "Oh, that our little sister would but come! then we should be free."

When the little girl heard this (for she stood behind the door all the time and listened), she ran forward, and in an instant all the ravens took their right form again; and all hugged and kissed each other, and went merrily home.

KING
THRUSHBEARD

A king had a daughter who was beautiful beyond all measure, but so proud and haughty withal that no suitor was good enough for her. She sent away one after another, and ridiculed them as well.

Once, the king made a great feast and invited thereto, from far and near, all the young men likely to marry. They were all marshaled in a row according to their rank and standing: first came the kings; then the grand dukes; then the princes, the earls, the barons, and the gentry.

Then the king's daughter was led through the ranks, but to every suitor she had some objection to make: one was too fat; "The wine-cask," she said. Another was too tall: "Long and thin has little in." The third was too short: "Short and thick is never quick." The fourth was too pale: "As pale as death." The fifth was too red: "A fighting-cock." The sixth was not straight enough: "A green log dried behind the stove." So she had something to say against every one, but she made herself especially merry over a good king who stood quite

high up in the row, and whose chin had grown a little crooked. "Well," she cried, and laughed, "he has a chin like a thrush's beak!" and from that time he got the name King Thrushbeard. But the old king, when he saw that his daughter did nothing but mock the people, and despised all the suitors who were gathered there, was very angry, and swore that she should have for her husband the very first beggar that came to his door.

143

144

When they came to a large forest, she asked,
  "To whom does that beautiful forest belong?"
  He replied, "It belongs to King Thrushbeard;
if you had taken him, it would have been yours."
  "Ah, unhappy girl that I am, if I had but taken
King Thrushbeard!" she said.

Afterward they came to a meadow, and she asked again,
   "To whom does this beautiful green meadow belong?"
   He replied, "It belongs to King Thrushbeard;
if you had taken him, it would have been yours."
   "Ah, unhappy girl that I am, if I had but taken
King Thrushbeard!" she said.

Then they came to a large town, and she asked again,
   "To whom does this fine large town belong?"
   He replied, "It belongs to King Thrushbeard;
if you had taken him, it would have been yours."
   "Ah, unhappy girl that I am, if I had but taken
King Thrushbeard!" she said.

"It does not please me," said the fiddler, "to hear you always wishing for another husband; am I not good enough for you?"

At last they came to a very little hut, and she said, "Oh, goodness! What a small house; to whom does this miserable, tiny hovel belong?"

The fiddler answered, "That is my house and yours, where we shall live together."

For a few days they lived in this way as well as might be, and came to the end of all their provisions. Then the man said, "Wife, we cannot go on any longer eating and drinking here and earning nothing. You must make baskets." He went out, cut some willows, and brought them home. Then she began to weave, but the tough willows wounded her delicate hands.

"I see that this will not do," said the man. "You had better spin; perhaps you can do that better." She sat down and tried to spin, but the hard thread soon cut her soft fingers so that the blood ran down. "See," said the man, "you are fit for no sort of work; I have made a bad bargain with you. Now I will try to make a business with pots and earthenware; you must sit in the marketplace and sell the wares." "Alas," thought she, "if any of the people from my father's kingdom come to the market and see me sitting there, selling, how they will mock me!" But it was of no use; she had to yield unless she chose to die of hunger.

For the first time she succeeded well, for the people were glad to buy the woman's wares because she was good-looking, and they paid her what she asked; many even gave her the money and left the pots with her as well. So they lived on what she had earned as long as it lasted. Then the husband bought a lot of new crockery. With this she sat down at the corner of the marketplace, and set it out round about her, ready for sale.

But suddenly there came a drunken hussar galloping along, and he rode right among the pots so that they were all broken into a thousand bits. The king's daughter began to weep, and did not know what to do for fear. "Alas! What will happen to me?" cried she. "What will my husband say to this?" She ran home and told him of the misfortune.

"Who would seat herself at a corner of the marketplace with crockery?" said the man. "Leave off crying; I see very well that you cannot do any ordinary work, so I have been to our king's palace and have asked whether they cannot find a place for a kitchen-maid, and they have promised to take you; in that way you will get your food for nothing."

The king's daughter was now a kitchen-maid, and had to be at the cook's beck and call, and do the dirtiest work. In each of her pockets she fastened a little jar, in which she took home her share of the leavings, and upon this they lived.

One day it happened that the wedding of the king's eldest son was to be celebrated, so the poor woman went up and placed herself by the door of the hall to look on. When all the candles were lit, and people, each more beautiful than the one before, entered, and all was full of pomp and splendor, she thought of her lot with a sad heart, and cursed the pride and haughtiness that had humbled her and brought her to such great poverty.

The smell of the delicious dishes that were being taken in and out reached her, and now and then the servants threw her a few morsels; these she put in her jars to take home.

All at once the king's son entered, clothed in velvet and silk, with gold chains about his neck. And when he saw the beautiful woman standing by the door he seized her by the hand, and would have danced with her, but she refused and shrank with fear, for she saw that it was King Thrushbeard, the suitor whom she had driven away with scorn.

163

Her struggles were of no avail; he drew her into the hall, but the string by which her pockets were hung broke, the pots fell down, the soup ran out, and the scraps were scattered all about. And when the people saw it, there arose general laughter and derision, and the king's daughter was so ashamed that she would rather have been a thousand fathoms below the ground.

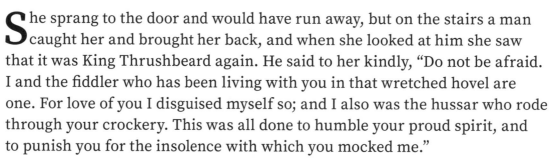

She sprang to the door and would have run away, but on the stairs a man caught her and brought her back, and when she looked at him she saw that it was King Thrushbeard again. He said to her kindly, "Do not be afraid. I and the fiddler who has been living with you in that wretched hovel are one. For love of you I disguised myself so; and I also was the hussar who rode through your crockery. This was all done to humble your proud spirit, and to punish you for the insolence with which you mocked me."

Then she wept bitterly and said, "I have done great wrong, and am not worthy to be your wife." But he said, "Be comforted; the evil days are past. Now we will celebrate our wedding."

Then the maids-in-waiting came and put on her the most splendid clothing, and her father and his whole court came and wished her happiness in her marriage with King Thrushbeard, and the joy now began in earnest. I wish you and I had been there, too.

TOM THUMB

There was once a poor countryman who used to sit in the chimney corner all evening and poke the fire, while his wife sat at her spinning wheel.

And he used to say, "How dull it is without any children about us; our house is so quiet, and other people's houses are so noisy and merry!"

"Yes," answered his wife, and sighed. "If we could only have one, and that one ever so little, no bigger than my thumb, how happy I should be! It would, indeed, be having our heart's desire."

Now, it happened that after a while the woman had a child who was perfect in all his limbs, but no bigger than a thumb. Then the parents said, "He is just what we wished for, and we will love him very much," and they named him according to his stature, Tom Thumb. And though they gave him plenty of nourishment, he grew no bigger, but remained exactly the same size as when he was first born; and he had very good faculties, and was very quick and prudent, so that all he did prospered.

One day his father made ready to go
into the forest to cut wood, and he said,
as if to himself, "Now, I wish there was
someone to bring the cart to meet me."

"Oh, Father," cried Tom Thumb, "I can
bring the cart, let me alone for that, and
in proper time, too!"

Then the father laughed, and said,
"How will you manage that? You are much
too little to hold the reins."

"That has nothing to do with it, Father;
while my mother goes on with her spinning
I will sit in the horse's ear and tell him where
to go."

"Well," answered the father, "we will try
it for once."

When it was time to set off, the mother
went on spinning, after setting Tom Thumb
in the horse's ear; and so he drove off, crying,
"Gee-up, gee-woo!"

So the horse went on quite as if his master were driving him, and drew the wagon along the right road to the wood.

Now it happened just as they turned a corner, and the little fellow was calling out "Gee-up!" that two strange men passed by.

"Look," said one of them, "how is this? There goes a wagon, and the driver is calling to the horse, and yet he is nowhere to be seen."

"It is very strange," said the other. "We will follow the wagon, and see where it belongs."

And the wagon went right through the wood, up to the place where the wood had been hewed.

When Tom Thumb caught sight of his father, he cried out, "Look, Father, here am I with the wagon; now, take me down."

The father held the horse with his left hand, and with the right he lifted down his little son out of the horse's ear, and Tom Thumb sat down on a stump, quite happy and content.

When the two strangers saw him they were struck dumb with wonder. At last one of them, taking the other aside, said to him, "Look here, the little chap would make our fortune if we were to show him in the town for money. Suppose we buy him."

So they went up to the woodcutter, and said, "Sell the little man to us; we will take care he shall come to no harm."

"No," answered the father; "he is the apple of my eye, and not for all the money in the world would I sell him."

But Tom Thumb, when he heard what was going on, climbed up by his father's coattails, and, perching himself on his shoulder, he whispered in his ear, "Father, you might as well let me go. I will soon come back again."

Then the father gave him up to the two men for a large piece of money.

They asked him where he would like to sit. "Oh, put me on the brim of your hat," said he. "There I can walk about and view the country, and be in no danger of falling off."

So they did as he wished, and when Tom Thumb had taken leave of his father, they set off all together. And they traveled on until it grew dusk, and the little fellow asked to be set down a little while for a change, and after some difficulty they consented. So the man took him down from his hat, and set him in a field by the roadside, and he ran away directly, and, after creeping about among the furrows, he slipped suddenly into a mouse-hole, just what he was looking for.

"Good evening, my masters, you can go home without me!" cried he to them, laughing. They ran up and felt about with their sticks in the mouse-hole, but in vain. Tom Thumb crept farther and farther in, and as it was growing dark, they had to make the best of their way home, full of vexation, and with empty purses.

When Tom Thumb found they were gone, he crept out of his hiding-place underground. "It is dangerous work groping about these holes in the darkness," said he. "I might easily break my neck."

But by good fortune he came upon an empty snail shell. "That's all right," said he. "Now I can get safely through the night;" and he settled himself down in it. Before he had time to get to sleep, he heard two men pass by, and one was saying to the other, "How can we manage to get hold of the rich parson's gold and silver?"

"I can tell you how," cried Tom Thumb.

"How is this?" said one of the thieves, quite frightened. "I hear someone speak!"

So they stood still and listened, and Tom Thumb spoke again. "Take me with you; I will show you how to do it!"

"Where are you, then?" asked they.

"Look about on the ground and notice where the voice comes from," answered he.

At last they found him, and lifted him up.

"You little elf," said they, "how can you help us?"

"Look here," answered he. "I can easily creep between the iron bars of the parson's room and hand out to you whatever you would like to have."

"Very well," said they, "we will try what you can do."

So when they came to the parsonage-house, Tom Thumb crept into the room, but cried out with all his might, "Will you have all that is here?" So the thieves were terrified, and said, "Do speak more softly, lest anyone should be awakened."

But Tom Thumb made as if he did not hear them, and cried out again, "What would you like? Will you have all that is here?" so that the cook, who was sleeping in a room nearby, heard it, and raised herself in bed and listened. The thieves, however, in their fear of being discovered, had run back part of the way, but they took courage again, thinking that it was only a jest of the little fellow's. So they came back and whispered to him to be serious, and to hand them out something. Then Tom Thumb called out once more as loud as he could, "Oh yes, I will give it all to you, only put out your hands." Then the listening maid heard him distinctly that time, and jumped out of bed, and burst open the door. The thieves ran off as if the wild huntsman were behind them; but the maid, as she could see nothing, went to fetch a light. And when she came back with one, Tom Thumb had taken himself off, without being seen by her, into the barn; and the maid, when she had looked in every hole and corner and found nothing, went back to bed at last, and thought that she must have been dreaming with her eyes and ears open.

So Tom Thumb crept among the hay, and found a comfortable nook to sleep in, where he intended to remain until it was day, and then to go home to his father and mother. But other things were to befall him; indeed, there is nothing but trouble and worry in this world!

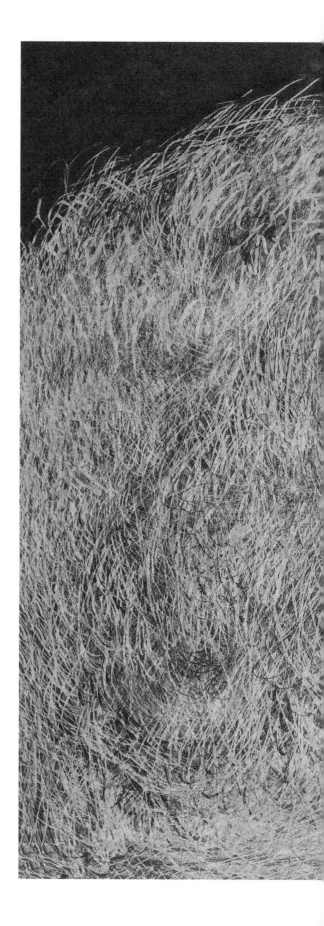

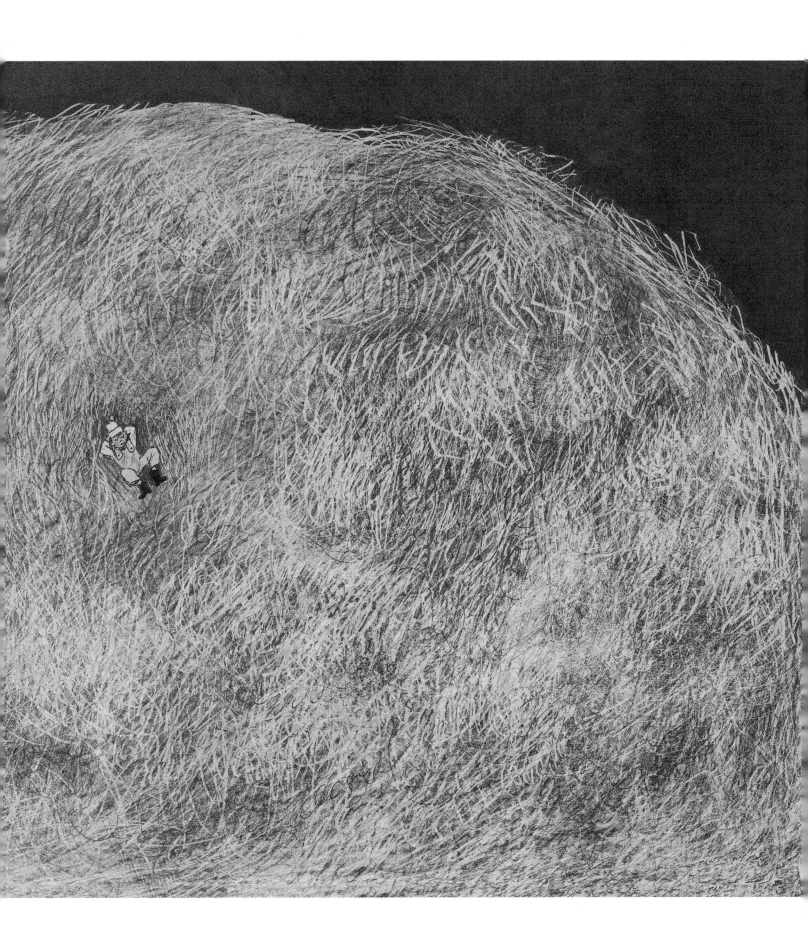

The maid got up at dawn to feed the cows. The first place she went to was the barn, where she took up an armful of hay, and it happened to be the very heap in which Tom Thumb lay asleep. And he was so fast asleep, that he was aware of nothing, and never awoke until he was in the mouth of the cow, who had taken him up with the hay.

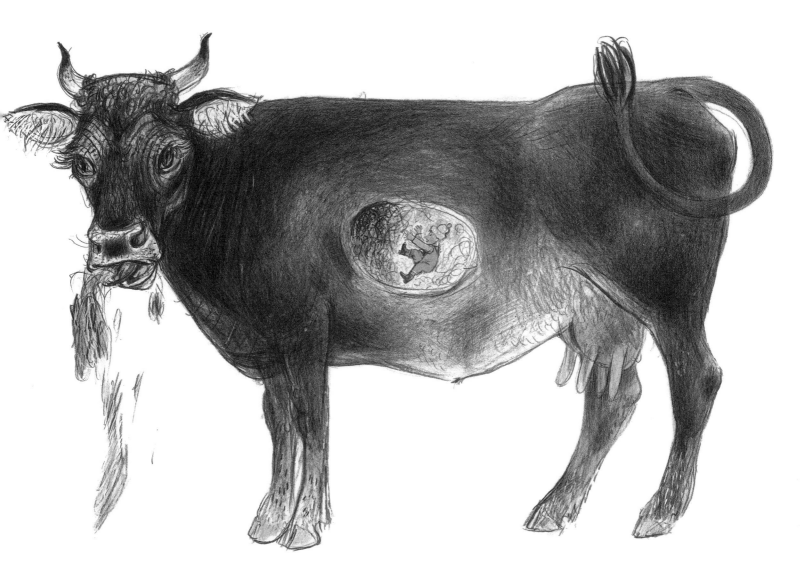

The maid was then milking the cow, and as she heard a voice, but could see no one, and as it was the same voice that she had heard in the night, she was so frightened that she fell off her stool, and spilled the milk. Then she ran in great haste to her master, crying, "Oh, master dear, the cow spoke!" "You must be crazy," answered her master, and he went himself to the cow-house to see what was the matter. No sooner had he put his foot inside the door, than Tom Thumb cried out again, "No more hay for me! No more hay for me!" Then the parson himself was frightened, supposing that a bad spirit had entered into the cow, and he ordered her to be put to death. So she was killed, but the stomach, where Tom Thumb was lying, was thrown upon a dunghill.

Tom Thumb had great trouble to work his way out of it, and he had just made a space big enough for his head to go through, when a new misfortune happened. A hungry wolf ran up and swallowed the whole stomach at one gulp. But Tom Thumb did not lose courage. "Perhaps," thought he, "the wolf will listen to reason," and he cried out from the inside of the wolf, "My dear wolf, I can tell you where to get a splendid meal!"

"Where is it to be had?" asked the wolf.

"In such and such a house, and you must creep into it through the drain, and there you will find cakes and bacon and broth, as much as you can eat," and he described to him his father's house. The wolf needed not to be told twice. He squeezed himself through the drain in the night, and feasted in the storeroom to his heart's content.

When, at last, he was satisfied, he wanted to go away again, but he had become so big, that to creep the same way back was impossible. This Tom Thumb had reckoned upon, and began to make a terrible din inside the wolf, crying and calling as loud as he could.

"Will you be quiet?" said the wolf; "you will wake the folks up!" "Look here," cried the little man, "you are very well satisfied, and now I will do something for my own enjoyment," and began again to make all the noise he could. At last the father and mother were awakened, and they ran to the room-door and peeped through the chink, and when they saw a wolf in occupation, they ran and fetched weapons—the man an axe, and the wife a scythe.

"Stay behind," said the man, as they entered the room; "when I have given him a blow, and it does not seem to have killed him, then you must cut at him with your scythe."

Then Tom Thumb heard his father's voice, and cried, "Dear father, I am here in the wolf's inside."

Then the father called out full of joy, "Thank heaven that we have found our dear child!" and told his wife to keep the scythe out of the way, lest Tom Thumb should be hurt with it.

Then he drew near and struck the wolf such a blow on the head that he fell down dead; and then he fetched a knife and a pair of scissors, slit up the wolf's body, and let out the little fellow.

"Oh, what anxiety we have felt about you!" said the father.

"Yes, Father, I have seen a good deal of the world, and I am very glad to breathe fresh air again." "And where have you been all this time?" asked his father.

"Oh, I have been in a mouse-hole and a snail's shell, in a cow's stomach and a wolf's inside: now, I think, I will stay at home." "And we will not part with you for all the kingdoms of the world," cried the parents, as they kissed and hugged their dear little Tom Thumb. And they gave him something to eat and drink, and a new suit of clothes, as his old ones were soiled with travel.

HANS IN LUCK

Retold by Felix Hoffmann

Hans had served his master for seven years, so he said to him, "Master, my time is up. Now I would like to go back home to my mother. Give me my wages." The master answered, "You have served me faithfully and honestly. As the service was, so shall the reward be." And he gave Hans a piece of gold as big as his head.

Hans pulled his handkerchief out of his pocket, wrapped the lump of gold
in it, put it on his shoulder, and set out on his way home. As he went,
he saw a horseman. "Ah," said Hans, quite loudly, "what a fine thing it is to
ride. There you sit as on a chair, never stumbling over a stone, saving your
shoes, and making your way without even knowing it."

The rider stopped and called out, "I will tell you what. Let's trade. I will give
you my horse, and you can give me your lump."

The rider got down, took the gold, and helped Hans up. Hans was heartily delighted as he sat upon the horse and rode away so bold and free.

After a little while he thought that it ought to go faster, and he began to call out, "Jup, jup."

Before Hans knew where he was, he was thrown off and lying in a ditch.
The horse would have escaped if it had not been stopped by a peasant,
who was coming along the road and driving a cow before him.

Hans said to the peasant, "Never again will I mount this horse.
Now, I like your cow, for one can walk quietly behind her, and moreover
have one's milk, butter, and cheese every day without fail."

"What would I not give to have such a cow?"
"Well," said the peasant, "I do not mind trading the cow for the horse."

Hans agreed with the greatest delight, and the peasant jumped upon the horse
and rode quickly away.

Hans drove his cow quietly before him. He felt very hot, and his tongue
stuck to the roof of his mouth with thirst. "I will milk the cow now and refresh
myself with the milk."

But the cow was old and not a drop of milk came. And because he was working in a clumsy way, the impatient beast gave him such a blow on his head with its hind foot that he fell to the ground.

A butcher came along the road just then with a young pig. "Well, well," said Hans, "to have a young pig like that! What meat one has! And there are sausages as well."

"Listen, Hans," said the butcher. "To do you a favor, I will trade, and let you have the pig for the cow." The pig was unbound from the cart, and the cord by which it was tied was put in his hand. Hans gave the cow to the butcher and held onto the rope with the pig.

Hans went on, thinking to himself how everything was going just as he wished. Presently, he was joined by a lad who was carrying a fine white goose under his arm.

Hans thought, "from a goose you get feathers and a good roast as well."
He said, "Let's trade."

As he was walking on with the goose, there stood a scissors grinder with his cart, singing a song. Hans said: "All's well with you, as you are so merry with your grinding."

"You must become a grinder, as I am. Then all will be well with you too. Here is a whetstone for you. Give me the goose in exchange."

And he gave him a fieldstone as well. Hans loaded himself with the stones and went on with a contented heart, his eyes shining with joy.

He came to a well in a field, where he wanted to drink. He laid the stones carefully by his side on the edge of the well. Then he pushed against the stones, and both of them fell into the water.

Hans jumped for joy, and then knelt down, and with tears in his eyes thanked God for having shown him this favor also, and delivered him in so good a way from those heavy stones, which had been the only things that troubled him.

"No one under the sun is as fortunate as I am," he cried out. With a light heart and free from every burden he now ran on until he was at home with his mother.

FELIX HOFFMANN

Felix Hoffmann was born in 1911 in Aarau, Switzerland, the son of a music teacher. For a short time he attended technical school in Basel and then went on to study at the Baden State Art College in Karlsruhe, Germany, and the United State College for Fine and Applied Arts in Berlin. During his studies he met his future wife, Gretel Kienscherf, and they had four children.

In addition to his activities as an artist, he was an assistant art teacher at the regional school in Aarau from 1935 to 1961. From 1955 until his death, he worked in his Hasenberg studio in Aarau, where he received visitors from all over the world who were interested in his art and books. He often said, "Anyone who makes books will get along with people, no matter where he lives."

The main focus of Hoffmann's many-sided creativity was book illustration and glass painting. In all, he illustrated eighty-six books. The fairy-tale picture books were produced between 1949 and 1975. All these volumes were published in many different countries, including the United States and Japan, and many of them were bestsellers.

Hoffmann also received numerous commissions for glass paintings in public buildings, such as the colorful choir window in Aarau's town church, windows in the Aarau town hall and the canton library, and the Isaiah window in the Bern Minster. He also painted murals, frescoes, and sgrafitti. The best known of these is the "Dance of Death" in the Upper Tower in Aarau (1966). He also created a substantial number of lithographs, etchings, and drawings.

In 1957, Hoffmann was awarded the Swiss Children's Book Prize for his life's work. He also appeared on the Honors list for the Hans Christian Andersen Award several times, and in 1972 he was short-listed for the same award for his life's work.

Felix Hoffmann died in 1975. Together with Hans Fischer (known as Fis) and Alois Carigiet, he is recognized as one of the most important twentieth-century Swiss illustrators of children's books.

AFTERWORD

How timely it is that the illustrations of Felix Hoffmann are brought back into view through this welcome publication of his interpretations of classic tales. Hoffmann deserves to be considered one of the great book illustrators of his generation. The delicate sensitivity of his draftsmanship teases out warmth and humanity while never sanitizing the darker side of the texts. Hoffmann was a designer in every sense of the word. His experience of designing for other media and processes, such as glass engraving, gave him a particular concern for surface. His skills as a printmaker, and consequent close concern for the means by which his work would be reproduced, explain the richness and depth that are achieved through his layering of color and texture. These technical skills underpinned a unique visual vocabulary that makes his work so instantly recognizable. Hoffmann was a master of scale, as is so evident in the image of the sorceress towering threateningly over the husband in "Rapunzel" or of Tom Thumb disappearing into an ocean of hay. And his ability to communicate tenderness was unparalleled, exemplified by his portrayal of the gentle embrace of Rapunzel and the prince in the tower. But Hoffmann's range virtuosity as a draftsman is so great that we find ourselves as convinced by his anthropomorphic goats in "The Wolf and the Seven Little Kids" as we are by the sublime landscapes through which the story of "The Seven Ravens" unfolds.

This magnificent collection of Hoffmann's works reminds us that whether placing his characters in a detailed atmospheric landscape or making them dance across the empty white of the page, Felix Hoffmann was always in complete control of his "stage": the pages of the book.

Martin Salisbury
Professor of Illustration at Cambridge School of Art, Anglia Ruskin University

EDITORIAL NOTE

When asked what he hoped to achieve with his work for children, Felix Hoffmann once replied, "As a children's book artist I have no other purpose than to tell the children a story and give them pleasure, and above all I have no ulterior educational motive."

Originally, Hoffmann illustrated the picture books of the Grimm brothers' fairy tales just for his family and not for publication. The style is notable for its sparing use of color, clear composition, atmospheric landscapes, and rich details. In his portrayal of the characters, Hoffmann attached great importance to making them lifelike, and he always brought out their individual human features. He was also very keen to ensure that children spent some time gazing at the pictures so that they could keep discovering new details in them.

In two of the tales, Hoffmann diverged from the original texts of the Brothers Grimm. One of these was "Hans in Luck," in which the illustrations were confined to just the main characters, and the text was correspondingly shortened. The other was "Rapunzel." Hoffmann frequently told these fairy tales to his children simply as they came into his head, without even looking up the Grimm versions. And his children always insisted that he should tell the tales in exactly the same way. The first publisher wanted to publish "Rapunzel" just as Hoffmann always told it. And so he made twenty lithograph pictures, and they were duly printed. Then the text was to be added, but to his surprise Hoffmann discovered that the end of the original story was different from that in his printed pictures. He had a bad conscience, but there was nothing else he could do except "compose" the text himself. Some experts on the subject criticized Hoffmann and even accused him of deliberately desexing the story because there is no mention in his version of Rapunzel giving birth to twins. However, this was absolutely unintentional on Hoffmann's part. He added the ending, in which a large crow takes the witch away for its chicks to eat, purely in response to his children asking, "What happened to the witch?"

Many years later, Hoffmann was amazed and delighted to learn that his ending actually corresponded to the Balkans version of the story.

The present publisher has deliberately opted to use Hoffmann's versions of "Rapunzel" and "Hans in Luck" in order to match text and pictures.

FIRST GERMAN PUBLICATION OF THE FAIRY-TALE PICTURE BOOKS

RAPUNZEL
Amerbach Verlag, Basel, 1949

THE WOLF AND THE SEVEN LITTLE KIDS
Verlag H.R. Sauerländer & Co, Aarau/Frankfurt, 1957

SLEEPING BEAUTY
Verlag H.R. Sauerländer & Co, Aarau/Frankfurt, 1959

THE SEVEN RAVENS
Verlag H.R. Sauerländer & Co, Aarau/Frankfurt, 1962

KING THRUSHBEARD
Verlag H.R. Sauerländer & Co, Aarau/Frankfurt, 1969

TOM THUMB
Verlag H.R. Sauerländer & Co, Aarau/Frankfurt, 1972

HANS IN LUCK
Verlag H.R. Sauerländer & Co, Aarau/Frankfurt, 1975

Imprint

© 2017 by NordSüd Verlag AG, CH-8005 Zürich, Switzerland.
First published in Switzerland by NordSüd Verlag under the title
"Hans Im Glück und andere Märchen der Brüder Grimm"
English edition copyright © 2017 by NorthSouth Books Inc., New York 10016.
Afterword copyright © 2017 by Martin Salisbury

First published in the United States, Great Britain, Canada, Australia, and New Zealand in 2017 by
NorthSouth Books Inc., an imprint of NordSüd Verlag AG, CH-8005 Zürich, Switzerland.

Distributed in the United States by NorthSouth Books Inc., New York 10016.
Library of Congress Cataloging-in-Publication Data is available.

ISBN: 978-0-7358-4281-6 (trade)
Printed in Germany by Grafisches Centrum Cuno GmbH & Co. KG
1 3 5 7 9 · 10 8 6 4 2
www.northsouth.com

Sponsored by:

Little Red Riding Hood
"My what big talent she has!"— Kirkus Reviews

The Three Little Pigs
"A marvelous offering that begs to be added
to everyone's storytelling repertoire."— School Library Journal

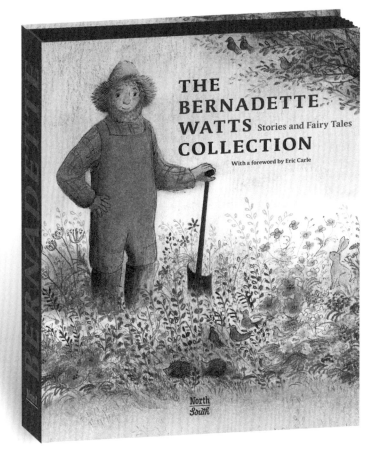

The Bernadette Watts Collection
Stories and Fairy Tales
With a foreword by Eric Carle
ISBN: 978-0-7358-4212-0

Thirty-eight timeless tales offer a visual treasure chest for the whole family!
From "Little Red Riding Hood," "Cinderella," and "The Three Little Pigs
to Snow White," "The Bremen Town Musicians," "The Ugly Duckling,"
and many more, acclaimed illustrator Bernadette Watts brings new life to these
beloved classics.

North
South

"At different times dramatic, pretty, comical, cartoonlike, stylized, and decorative, Leupin's always-polished illustrations … now collected into this single volume."
— Booklist

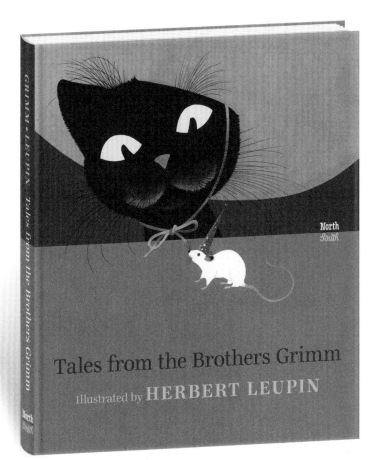

Tales from the Brothers Grimm
Illustrated by Herbert Leupin
With an afterword by arts journalist Sieglinde Geisel
ISBN: 978-0-7358-4228-1

World-renowned poster designer Herbert Leupin's bold, colorful illustrations offer a fresh take on nine favorite Grimms' fairy tales—"The Brave Little Tailor," "Hans in Luck," "Hansel and Gretel," "Puss in Boots," "Sleeping Beauty," and more—imbuing each with the humor and innovation, graphic simplicity, and colorful palette for which his posters and designs are famous. This treasure is a visual feast for all!

relaxed cooking

with curtis stone

recipes to put you in my favorite mood

curtis stone
photographs by quentin bacon

Clarkson Potter/Publishers
New York

All rights reserved.
Published in the United States by Clarkson Potter/Publishers,
an imprint of the Crown Publishing Group, a division of Random House, Inc., New York.
www.crownpublishing.com
www.clarksonpotter.com

CLARKSON POTTER is a trademark and POTTER
with colophon is a registered trademark of Random House, Inc.

Library of Congress Cataloging-in-Publication Data
Stone, Curtis.
   Relaxed cooking with Curtis Stone / Curtis Stone.—1st ed.
      p.   cm.
   Includes index.
   1. Cookery.   I. Title.
   TX714.S786   2009
   641.5—dc22   2008036992

ISBN 978-0-307-40874-7

Printed in China

Design by Subtitle
Photography by Quentin Bacon

10 9 8 7 6 5 4 3 2 1

First Edition

contents

introduction

Being relaxed comes pretty naturally to me. What can I say? I'm an Aussie—we're just made that way. For me, there are few things that are more relaxing than lingering at the table with good friends, finishing off a bottle of wine while scraping the last few crumbs of dessert off my plate or sopping up some delicious sauce from the bottom of a serving bowl with a crust of bread amid laughter and good conversation. But I know that for a lot of people, putting together a meal, especially for guests, is the opposite of relaxing—it's a stressful, time- and labor-intensive undertaking that leaves the kitchen a wreck and nerves frayed. I'm here to tell you: It doesn't have to be that way.

Food has always been at the center of my world. Some of my earliest and best memories revolve around food: Sundays sharing hearty roast dinners with my grandparents, being spoiled with fish and chips at my dad's place on Friday nights, Mum removing a thorn from my stained hands after a day's blackberry-picking, or a simple barbecue with my brother and a few mates. I'll never forget the first time I ate in a fancy restaurant and experienced a five-star meal and how great food could taste. I was hooked. Looking back, I guess I always knew I was going to be a chef.

I started cooking in a restaurant as soon as I left school, working and training for four years in my hometown of Melbourne, Australia, before I set sail to experience the cuisines of Europe. There I had the privilege of cooking with some of the best chefs in the world and even served as head chef in a couple of London's finest restaurants. When I think back on all my amazing food experiences, though, the ones I remember most fondly are not gala productions with multiple courses and showy presentations, but the meals where everything came together in a relaxed way and my guests felt as much at home and as comfortable as I did. I love to eat in great restaurants, but I truly think that the most memorable meals are served at home. Let's face it: At home, you are comfortable. When I'm home I can play my favorite music, have my shoes off if I want, and stay up as late as I like. And when I'm that comfortable, everything seems to taste a little bit better.

Of course, in a perfect world you would be as relaxed when you are planning the menu and cooking the meal as you are when you are gathered around the table. You don't have to be a great cook to put good food on the table—all you really need to do is to get your hands on quality ingredients and treat them simply. Remember that rule, and, honestly, you can't go wrong.

When Mother Nature worked out what we should be eating at different times of the year, she did a pretty good job, so listen to her. Food that is in season just tastes better. It is always less expensive, and chances are it hasn't been artificially treated or traveled halfway across the world to reach your kitchen. Consequently, when you buy seasonal produce it is usually a lot healthier, you are not contributing to climate change or global warming through carbon emissions and wasted fuel, and you are supporting your local farmers and community.

When I first moved to the States, I looked forward to going to the market, as there were so many new ingredients that I had never used before. It was like starting a whole new food adventure, and I had lots of interesting conversations about what I found. If you generally frequent the same markets, it's worth your while to befriend the people who work there. I love to see the smiles on people's faces when I show an interest in their profession. Asking my local fish guy where the dorade comes from instantly stirs a conversation, and when I ask him how many fish he had filleted that morning, I see his chest puff up when he replies, "Wow, I lost count at thirty." By having a laugh with these men and women, you not only learn a bunch but you also put a little sparkle in their day. Best of all, you'll get home with a lot of wonderful ingredients you can transform into truly delicious meals with very little effort.

To help my guests get in a relaxed mood as well, I always leave a couple of jobs for them to help with. You know how the first thing people ask when they walk through the door is "Is there anything I can do to help?" I always answer by saying "Yeah, would you mind opening the wine?" or "Fancy helping me shell these peas?" Getting people involved makes them feel at home. I also like to have a cocktail mixed up and ready to go, or to appoint a guest to make drinks, so everyone can get in the party spirit without my having to play bartender and chef all at once.

When it comes time to serve, I also get people involved carrying platters and plates of food to the table. I love to share food by passing it around the table from person to person, allowing guests to serve one another.

Lastly, make sure the conversation flows as freely as the food and drink. When I was a little boy, my mum would make us play a game at the dinner table called "best and worst." We would take turns talking about the best thing that had happened to us that day, followed by the worst thing. The conversation that ensued was always amazing, and I observe this tradition at my own table to this day—especially when there are children at the table. It's always fun to hear a kid's interpretation of their day.

Being relaxed is not simply a feeling; it's a state of mind. It's the sensation you get when you hear the crackle of an open fire, the feeling of the warmth from its flames, the smell from the charred wood, the mesmerizing glow that your eyes won't leave, and, of course, the taste of the marshmallow that you are slowly roasting over its coals. Each of the recipes in this book is designed to be simple and delicious, and to deliver a lot of flavor and plate appeal for the effort invested—in other words, to help you be as relaxed in the kitchen as you are in front of that crackling fire.

chapter one
first thing in the morning

The first thing you eat each day is often the most important. We all know that food is our fuel; its job at the start of each day is to give us energy for what lies ahead. During the night you can become dehydrated, and so you need to replenish yourself with lots of fresh fruits and juices—dry toast and coffee just don't do the trick. I feel really strongly that you need to start the day with things that boost your metabolism and give a kick of instant energy without filling you up—even if you are going to follow with a more substantial breakfast.

Of course, we're all busy, and quite often we barely have time to eat breakfast, let alone cook one, so I've kept the recipes in this chapter super quick and easy. Several of the dishes, like the Tropical Smoothie, can be made in less than ten minutes or, like the granola, can be made in batches on the weekend. Do what you can when you have a bit more time—cut up fruit, poach the compote—so that when you run down in the morning, it's all there. You don't want to default to a cup of coffee, which will give you artificial energy only to leave you flat by the time you reach the office.

Even when I'm having a leisurely day and have a bit more time on my hands, I still like to ease into the morning with something fresh and light. I may spoil myself an hour or so later by cooking a more indulgent brunch or lunch, but I find, and I'm sure you will too, that starting the day with something fresh and healthful not only helps to wake me up but also places me in a great frame of mind, setting the mood for the rest of the day.

berry good
start to the day

Berries have so much inherent sweetness that they are the perfect thing to get you going in the a.m. because they give you a burst of natural energy. It takes just seconds to turn them into a drink, and you don't even need to get out the blender. I often hear people say, "Berries don't taste the way they used to." Just-picked ripe berries are fantastic; those that are grown in a hothouse and flown halfway around the world are not. Try to find berries that have been grown locally, are organic, preferably, and most important, are in season.

Serves 2

¾ cup (3 ounces)
fresh blackberries

¾ cup (3 ounces)
fresh raspberries

⅔ cup (3 ounces)
fresh blueberries

5 fresh strawberries,
hulled and quartered

½ lime, quartered

Crushed ice

⅔ cup cranberry juice cocktail

Combine all the berries and the lime in a mortar, and gently muddle with the pestle until the berries are coarsely smashed and exuding their juices. (Alternatively, blend the berries and lime in a food processor or blender.)

Fill 2 glasses halfway with crushed ice, and spoon the berry mixture over the ice. Pour the cranberry juice over the berry mixture, and serve.

poached dried fruit
with rose water and orange

I always have dried fruit in the pantry, so this is an easy thing to throw together on the weekend, giving me a no-work instant breakfast for the busy week ahead. The fruit goes from shriveled and dry to something luscious to serve over yogurt, muesli, or even just on its own. You can rehydrate dried fruits with differently flavored liquids to enhance their natural sweetness. The dried fruits can be poached on the weekend and stored in the fridge for six or seven days.

Serves 4

½ cup (3 ounces) dried apricots

½ cup (2 ounces) dried peaches

½ cup (2 ounces) dried apples

½ cup (2 ounces) dried pears

½ cup (3 ounces) dried dates

½ cup honey

3 tablespoons rose water
(see Note)

2 cinnamon sticks

Zest of 2 oranges, cut into fine julienne

½ teaspoon freshly grated nutmeg

1 vanilla bean, split lengthwise

Place the dried fruit in a large bowl and add enough cold water (about 4 cups) to cover the fruit by 1 inch. Cover with plastic wrap and let stand at room temperature overnight.

Strain the soaking liquid into a large heavy skillet, and set the rehydrated fruit aside. You should have about 3 cups of soaking liquid. Add the honey, rose water, cinnamon sticks, orange zest, and nutmeg to the soaking liquid. Scrape the seeds from the vanilla bean into the liquid, and then add the bean, too. Bring to a boil over high heat. Then simmer over medium heat for 15 minutes, or until the liquid has reduced by half.

Reduce the heat to medium-low, so the liquid is at a low simmer. Add the reserved rehydrated fruit and simmer for 15 minutes, or until the fruit is just softened but not mushy. Remove the skillet from the heat and let the fruit cool in the syrup. Store in a sealed container in the refrigerator for up to 1 week.

Note

Rose water is a distillate of rose petals, so adding a little to the poaching liquid makes you feel like you are smelling roses as you eat your breakfast—it's floral but not overpowering. Rose water is used widely in Asian and Middle Eastern cookery, so the easiest place to find it is in a specialty market that stocks Asian or Middle Eastern ingredients.

homemade granola

My granola is quite indulgent: It's full of nuts and seeds and all the tasty stuff that brings you energy. Eat it with fresh or poached fruits or simply with cold milk; either way, it's guaranteed to keep the hunger at bay until lunch, even if that's hours away. It will keep in an airtight container for a week, so make it in big batches. See the photo on page 11.

Makes about 6 cups

4 tablespoons (½ stick) unsalted butter

1 tablespoon ground cinnamon

1 tablespoon freshly grated nutmeg

½ teaspoon ground cloves

¼ cup honey

¼ cup pure maple syrup

¼ cup (packed) light brown sugar

2 cups rolled oats (not instant)

1 cup shelled pumpkin seeds

1 cup shelled sunflower seeds

1 cup whole almonds

½ cup dried cranberries

½ cup raisins

Preheat the oven to 350°F. Combine the butter, cinnamon, nutmeg, and cloves in a small heavy saucepan over medium heat, and stir for 1 minute or until the butter has completely melted. Add the honey, maple syrup, and brown sugar and stir for 2 minutes, or until the sugar dissolves and the mixture comes to a simmer. Set it aside.

Spray a large heavy baking sheet with nonstick cooking spray. Combine the oats, pumpkin seeds, sunflower seeds, and almonds in a large bowl. Drizzle the warm syrup over the oat mixture and toss to coat well. Transfer the oat mixture to the prepared baking sheet, forming an even layer. Bake, stirring occasionally, for 30 minutes, or until the mixture is dry.

Stir in the cranberries and raisins and continue baking for 10 minutes, or until the granola darkens slightly. (At this point the granola will still be soft, but as it cools it will become crunchy.) Transfer the baking sheet to a cooling rack and let the granola cool completely. It will set into chunks, so simply break it up into smaller bits.

tropical smoothie

Full of nutrients and flavor, this is a healthy start to the day. If I'm in a rush, I even take it with me on the road and enjoy it all the way to work. Whatever fruit you've got on hand works: Just pop it all in the blender, whiz it, and you're good to go.

Serves 6

½ pineapple, peeled, cored, and coarsely chopped (about 4 cups)

1 papaya, peeled, seeded, and coarsely chopped (about 2½ cups)

¼ cantaloupe, peeled, seeded, and coarsely chopped (about 2 cups)

1 mango, peeled, pitted, and coarsely chopped (about 2 cups)

2 kiwi fruits, peeled and coarsely chopped (about ¾ cup)

1½ cups fresh coconut water (see Note)

2 cups ice cubes

Place half of the chopped pineapple, papaya, cantaloupe, mango, and kiwi fruits in a blender. Add ¾ cup of the coconut water and 1 cup of the ice. Puree until smooth. Divide the smoothie among 3 tall glasses. Repeat with the remaining ingredients, and serve immediately.

Note
Young coconuts can be found in the produce department of good grocery stores, but if you can't find a fresh one, you can substitute canned or boxed coconut water (*not* milk).

peach and
mint iced tea

I love, love, love refreshing iced tea. Actually, though I call this tea, there's no tea anywhere near it (or caffeine for that matter). The peaches add a slightly sweet flavor to the refreshing mint.

Serves 4

1¼ (lightly packed) cups fresh mint leaves (from 3 bunches)

3 ripe peaches, pitted

4 cups ice cubes, crushed

Pour 6 cups water into a medium saucepan. Cover and bring to a boil over high heat. Remove from the heat and add 1 cup of the mint leaves. Cover and steep for 30 minutes to allow the mint to infuse the water. Then strain the mint tea into a pitcher, discarding the leaves, and refrigerate until cold.

Meanwhile, chop 2 of the peaches coarsely and place them in a blender. Puree until smooth, adding a couple tablespoons of the mint tea if necessary to help create the puree. Strain the peach puree through a fine-mesh sieve and chill the puree.

Thinly slice the remaining peach. In 4 tall glasses, layer the crushed ice, thin slices of peach, and the remaining ¼ cup mint leaves, filling the glasses about halfway. Divide the peach puree among the 4 glasses. Then stir in the chilled mint tea and serve immediately.

caramelized nectarines
with yogurt and honey

You can't imagine how good this is: The honey and sugar make a golden crust on the fruit, and the combination of hot nectarines and cold yogurt is fantastic. If you have some caramelized nectarines left over, they are just as good cold or mixed into a fruit salad.

Serves 4

4 nectarines, pitted and cut into quarters

½ cup (packed) light brown sugar

1 cup plain Greek yogurt

4 teaspoons organic honey

Preheat the oven to 500°F. Line a large heavy baking sheet with foil and spray the foil with nonstick cooking spray. Place the nectarines, cut side up, in the center of the prepared baking sheet, and sprinkle with the brown sugar. Roast, basting once with the melted brown sugar, for 25 minutes, or until the sugar caramelizes and the nectarines are golden and slightly softened.

Spoon the yogurt into 4 bowls and top with the warm roasted nectarines. Drizzle with the honey, and serve.

watermelon with fresh mint and lime

Watermelon is the best thing in the world to eat first thing in the morning because its high water content really helps to flush your body out. The lime-flavored sugar syrup holds well, so you can make it at the beginning of the week and mix it with freshly cut melon each morning.

Serves 6

⅓ cup sugar

Grated zest and juice of 1 lime

¼ cup thinly sliced fresh mint leaves

½ large oval watermelon

Stir the sugar, 2 tablespoons water, the lime zest, and 1½ tablespoons of the lime juice together in a small heavy saucepan over high heat until the sugar dissolves and the syrup comes to a boil. Let the syrup cool completely, and then refrigerate it until cold.

Strain the chilled syrup into a small bowl and stir in the mint. Allow the mint to infuse into the syrup for at least 5 minutes.

Place the watermelon, cut side down, on a work surface. Using a large sharp knife, cut the watermelon horizontally to form a 2-inch-thick slab. (Reserve the remaining watermelon for another use.) Trim away the rind, and then cut the slab into 2-inch chunks. Transfer the watermelon chunks to a large serving platter, keeping the chunks in a single layer and maintaining the shape of the slab. Pour the cold syrup over the watermelon, and serve.

chapter two
brunch that will
blow their minds

I have no idea who came up with the concept of creating an extra meal in the day, or why, but to the person who fused breakfast and lunch to invent brunch: I salute you—you're a bloody genius! After all, breakfast is an incredible meal, as is lunch, but having the freedom to combine the best of both in one is a cook's dream. Just as the options are endless, so too are the ways that you can enjoy brunch. By its very nature, it's designed to be a lazy meal filled with great conversation, a glance through the morning paper, and, of course, plenty of good coffee. If the sun is shining, I find that sitting outside with a couple of friends and a delicious but easy-to-make spread really starts the day right.

What follows is a mix of sweet and savory dishes. Whether it be the simplicity of the Lazy Asparagus Omelet or the sheer indulgence of homemade waffles with caramelized apples, these dishes can be enjoyed from ten in the morning until two in the afternoon, give or take. And whether you are cooking for one lucky person or a crowd, I guarantee that you're going to blow their minds.

cinnamon french toast with caramelized peaches

If you're looking for an awesome brunch dish that can be made with minimal effort, this is the recipe for you. Caramelized peaches really hit the spot, but you can use anything else in the fruit bowl if peaches aren't in season—try apples or bananas.

Serves 4

Caramelized peaches

½ cup sugar

4 peaches (about 1¼ pounds total), pitted, each cut into 8 wedges

3 tablespoons unsalted butter

French toast

6 large eggs

Four ½-inch-thick slices brioche bread

¼ cup sugar

2 teaspoons ground cinnamon

2 tablespoons (¼ stick) unsalted butter

⅓ cup crème fraîche, for serving

To prepare the caramelized peaches: Combine the sugar and ¼ cup water in a large heavy sauté pan over medium heat. Stir until the sugar dissolves and the liquid comes to a simmer. Then boil over medium-high heat without stirring, brushing down the sides of the pan with a wet pastry brush and swirling the pan occasionally to ensure that the syrup cooks evenly, for 6 minutes, or until the syrup begins to turn golden brown. Immediately remove the pan from the heat. Add the peaches and butter and swirl until the butter melts. Cook over medium heat for 2 minutes, or until the peaches are just tender. Set the peaches aside.

To make the French toast: Using a fork, beat the eggs in a 13 x 9-inch baking dish. Place the slices of brioche in the eggs and let stand, turning the slices once, for 5 minutes, or until the eggs are absorbed.

Stir the sugar and cinnamon together on a large plate; set it aside. Melt the butter on a large heavy griddle pan over medium heat. Add the brioche slices to the hot pan and cook for about 2 minutes per side, or until golden brown on the outside and heated through. Immediately place the hot French toast in the cinnamon-sugar and turn to coat completely.

Divide the French toast among 4 serving plates. Spoon the caramelized peaches over the French toast. Top with a dollop of crème fraîche, and serve.

crêpes with orange caramel and mascarpone

The mascarpone and caramel make the dish especially luscious. The crêpes are really very easy to make; the batter can be prepared a couple of days in advance to make life even easier.

Serves 4

Crêpes

1 cup all-purpose flour, sifted

1¼ cups whole milk

½ cup heavy cream

2 large eggs

4 teaspoons sugar

Pinch of salt

1 tablespoon unsalted butter

Sauce

2 oranges

½ cup pure maple syrup

4 tablespoons (½ stick) unsalted butter

2 tablespoons Grand Marnier or other orange liqueur

Filling

1 cup mascarpone cheese

To make the crêpes: Combine the flour, milk, cream, eggs, sugar, and salt in a blender and blend until smooth. Cover and set aside for 30 minutes. (If making ahead of time, refrigerate and bring to room temperature 30 minutes before using.)

Heat a crêpe pan or a heavy 8-inch nonstick sauté pan over medium-low heat. Dab some of the butter on a paper towel and wipe the pan with a little butter. Pour 3 tablespoons of the batter into the center of the pan and swirl to coat the bottom thinly. Cook for 1½ minutes, or until the edges are light brown. Loosen the edges gently with a silicone spatula and carefully turn the crêpe over. Continue cooking for about 1 minute, or until the bottom begins to brown in spots. Transfer to a plate. Repeat with the remaining batter, wiping the pan with butter as needed, and forming 8 crêpes in all.

To make the sauce: Zest the oranges and set the grated zest aside. Using a sharp knife, cut away the remaining skin and all the white pith from the oranges. Working over a bowl to catch any juices, cut between the membranes to release the orange segments, letting them drop into the bowl. Squeeze the orange juice from the membranes into the bowl.

Heat the maple syrup in a large heavy sauté pan over medium heat until it begins to simmer. Add the butter, the orange zest, and the orange juice (reserving the segments), and simmer over medium-low heat for 5 minutes, or until the sauce thickens slightly. Add the Grand Marnier and simmer for 2 minutes, or until the sauce thickens slightly again.

Spread a large spoonful of mascarpone over each crêpe and fold it in half. Place 2 folded crêpes on each of 4 plates. Add the orange segments to the hot orange sauce and swirl the pan gently to warm the oranges. Then spoon the sauce and oranges over the crêpes and serve.

crispy vegetable fritters

If you are on the hunt for ways to get the people in your life to eat more veggies, look no further. These crispy fritters taste like you're eating something naughty but they're packed with healthy vegetables. Put a big basket in the center of the table with a bunch of other brunch dishes, and watch them disappear. They're also a fantastic snack reheated in the microwave and served with a dollop of chutney, so make extras.

Makes 12

1 russet potato, peeled

1 carrot, peeled

1 zucchini, ends trimmed

1 onion, halved and very thinly sliced

2 teaspoons sea salt

2 large eggs

Freshly ground black pepper

1/3 cup olive oil

1 cup sour cream

1/4 bunch fresh dill, leaves coarsely chopped (about 1 1/2 tablespoons)

Using a mandoline or a julienne peeler, cut the potato, carrot, and zucchini lengthwise into long spaghetti-like strips. Toss the strips, the onion slices, and the sea salt together in a medium bowl. Let the vegetable mixture stand for 10 minutes, or until the salt has drawn out some of the moisture from the vegetables. Then place the vegetables in a colander to drain the excess moisture. Squeeze the vegetables between your hands to extract as much moisture as possible.

Using a fork, beat the eggs and 1/4 teaspoon black pepper in a large bowl to blend well. Add the vegetables and stir to coat them with the eggs.

Heat 1 1/2 tablespoons of the oil in a large heavy sauté pan over medium-high heat. Working in batches and using about 1/4 cup of the vegetable-egg batter for each fritter, spoon the batter into the hot pan and form thin patties about 3 inches in diameter. Fry for 4 minutes on each side, or until the fritters are golden and crisp on the outside. Using a metal spatula, transfer the fritters to paper towels to absorb any excess oil.

Meanwhile, stir the sour cream and dill together in a small bowl. Season to taste with black pepper.

Place the fritters on a platter and serve with the sour cream–dill sauce.

spanish frittata

This dish is super-easy and really versatile. Feta cheese gives this frittata a salty, sharper edge than the usual cheddar or Monterey Jack cheese, and it's packed with veggies. Serve it warm or at room temperature.

Serves 4

1 large red-skinned potato, cut into 1/2-inch pieces

2 tablespoons olive oil

Salt and freshly ground black pepper

6 button mushrooms, halved

1 red bell pepper, seeded and cut into 2-inch-long strips

1 shallot, coarsely chopped

1 zucchini, cut into 1-inch-long strips

12 large organic free-range eggs

6 cherry tomatoes, halved

3 ounces feta cheese, coarsely crumbled (about 1/2 cup)

Preheat the oven to 350°F. Fill the bottom of a vegetable steamer with about 1 inch of water. Cover, and bring the water to a simmer over medium heat. Add the potato pieces to the steamer basket, cover the pot, and steam for 12 minutes, or until a skewer meets just a bit of resistance when inserted into the center of a piece of potato. Remove the potatoes from the steamer and let them cool completely.

Heat the oil in a 12-inch nonstick ovenproof sauté pan over medium-high heat. Add the potatoes, sprinkle with salt and pepper to taste, and sauté for 2 minutes, or until the potatoes are tender and pale golden. Add the mushrooms, bell peppers, and shallots and cook for 4 minutes, or until the vegetables soften slightly. Stir in the zucchini and reduce the heat to medium-low.

Whisk the eggs, 1/2 teaspoon salt, and 1/2 teaspoon pepper in a large bowl to blend well. Pour the egg mixture over the vegetables in the sauté pan. Add the tomatoes and feta cheese, and cook without stirring for about 5 minutes, or until the egg mixture is almost set but the top is still loose. Transfer the pan to the oven and bake for 20 minutes, or until the center is just set. Using a silicone spatula, loosen the frittata from the pan. Then slide the frittata onto a plate, and serve.

raspberry muffins

I promise that these are muffins like none you've ever tasted before. The almond meal makes them moist and chewy, so they're the perfect snack for any time of day. Why not double the recipe and share the love? One caveat, though: Don't make these unless raspberries are in season. To my palate, hothouse berries have no flavor and are not worth the hefty price tag.

Makes 9

1 cup almond meal

1 cup confectioners' sugar, sifted, plus more for dusting

1/3 cup all-purpose flour, sifted

1/2 teaspoon salt

1/2 cup (1 stick) unsalted butter, melted

5 large egg whites

About 1 1/2 cups fresh raspberries

Preheat the oven to 350°F. Spray 9 cups of a nonstick muffin pan with nonstick cooking spray. Whisk the almond meal, the 1 cup confectioners' sugar, the flour, and the salt in a large bowl to blend. Stir in the melted butter.

Using an electric mixer, beat the egg whites in another large bowl for 1 minute, or until soft peaks form. Using a rubber spatula, gently fold the egg whites into the batter. Then gently fold 1 cup of the raspberries into the batter. Immediately divide the batter among the prepared muffin cups, filling the cups completely. Place 2 or 3 of the remaining raspberries atop each muffin.

Bake for 30 minutes, or until the muffins are pale golden and the tops spring back when touched. Let the muffins cool in the pan for 5 minutes. Then gently twist the muffins to release them from the pan and let them cool completely on a wire rack.

Sift confectioners' sugar over the muffins, and serve.

greek doughnuts

Here's a really lazy way of making doughnuts. There's no rolling or cutting—you just drop blobs of dough into the hot oil. Invite your guests into the kitchen to keep you company as you make them. I guarantee that not many of these sticky, sweet treats will make it all the way to the table.

Makes about 30

4 teaspoons active dry yeast

2¼ cups lukewarm water (about 110°F)

⅓ cup plus 1 teaspoon sugar

2 large eggs

4 cups all-purpose flour

1 teaspoon salt

Canola oil, for deep-frying

½ teaspoon ground cinnamon

⅓ cup honey

⅓ cup hazelnuts, toasted, skinned (page 89), and finely crushed

Combine the yeast, ½ cup of the lukewarm water, and the teaspoon of sugar in a medium bowl. Set aside for 10 minutes, or until the yeast dissolves. Then whisk in the eggs, followed by the remaining 1¾ cups lukewarm water. Mix in the flour and salt, stirring constantly with a wooden spoon until you have a very thick and sticky batter. Cover the bowl with a clean dishcloth and set it aside in a warm place for about 1½ hours, or until the batter has risen and doubled in size and small bubbles have formed.

Fill a large deep frying pan with enough oil to come halfway up the sides of the pan. Heat the oil over medium heat to 375°F. Meanwhile, combine the remaining ⅓ cup sugar and the cinnamon in a large bowl and set it aside.

Working in batches and using about 2 tablespoons of the batter for each doughnut, spoon the batter into the hot oil (you can cook about 6 doughnuts at a time). The batter will be very thick and sticky, so be careful not to splash the hot oil. Fry each batch for 5 to 8 minutes, or until the doughnuts puff and become golden brown. Turn them occasionally to help them brown evenly, and adjust the heat as needed to ensure that the oil does not get too hot.

Using a mesh skimmer or a slotted spoon, transfer the doughnuts to a baking sheet lined with paper towels to absorb the excess oil. Immediately toss the hot doughnuts in the cinnamon-sugar to coat. Transfer the coated doughnuts to a warm platter.

Meanwhile, heat the honey in a small saucepan over medium heat until it is hot.

Drizzle the hot honey over the doughnuts. Sprinkle with the crushed hazelnuts, and serve.

hotcakes with delicious blueberry compote

The ricotta in these hotcakes makes them as fluffy as a pillow. I am especially fond of blueberries in pancakes because as they warm with the heat of cooking, they burst and give up their juice, making the pancakes juicy and light. The fresh flavor of mint and the tang of crème fraîche keep these from being too sweet.

Serves 4

Blueberry compote

18 ounces fresh blueberries

¼ cup sugar

Grated zest and juice of 1 lemon

¼ cup coarsely chopped fresh mint leaves (optional)

Hotcakes

1 cup fresh ricotta cheese

4 large eggs, separated

¾ cup buttermilk, shaken

1 cup all-purpose flour

1½ teaspoons baking powder

Pinch of salt

¼ cup sugar

½ cup fresh blueberries

About 3 tablespoons unsalted butter

Butter, for serving

To make the blueberry compote: Combine the blueberries, sugar, lemon zest, and 2 tablespoons of the lemon juice in a medium saucepan over medium heat and cook for 2 minutes, or until the sugar dissolves. (Don't let the berries cook too long or they will become mushy and lose their beautiful shape.) Remove from the heat. Gently stir in the chopped mint if using. Keep warm.

To make the hotcakes: Whisk the ricotta and the egg yolks together in a large bowl to combine; then whisk in the buttermilk. Sift the flour, baking powder, and salt into the ricotta mixture. Stir with a whisk until just combined.

Using an electric mixer, beat the egg whites and sugar in a large bowl until stiff peaks form. Using a large rubber spatula, gently fold the egg whites through the batter in 2 batches. Gently fold the fresh blueberries into the batter.

Melt some butter on a hot griddle pan over medium-low heat. Ladle the batter onto the griddle (you should be able to fit 3 hotcakes at a time) and cook for about 3 minutes per side, or until the hotcakes puff, become golden brown, and are just cooked through.

Transfer the hotcakes to plates. Spoon the warm blueberry compote over the hotcakes, and then top with a dollop of butter. Serve immediately.

lazy asparagus omelet

One of my favorite parts of going on holiday is heading down each morning to the hotel's breakfast buffet. I always make a beeline for the omelet station—even a chef loves having someone else man the omelet pan sometimes! Back at home, I make this much easier version and find it has all the flavor of those yummy holiday omelets. Taleggio is a creamy cheese similar to Brie, with a slightly stronger flavor; it pairs really well with asparagus. Serve this with some hot, grainy toast.

Serves 4 to 6

15 thin asparagus spears (about 6 ounces total), tough ends trimmed

12 large eggs

1/2 teaspoon salt

1/2 teaspoon freshly ground black pepper

1 tablespoon unsalted butter

2 ounces Taleggio cheese, shaved into thin slices

Bring a medium saucepan of water to a boil over high heat. Cut the tips of the asparagus spears into 3-inch lengths; then cut the remainder of the spears into 1/4-inch-thick slices. Cook the asparagus in the boiling water for 30 seconds, or just until it becomes bright green. Drain the asparagus and submerge it in a large bowl of ice water until cool; drain again.

Preheat the broiler. Using a fork, whisk the eggs, salt, and pepper in a large bowl to blend well. Melt the butter in a 12-inch nonstick ovenproof sauté pan over medium heat, swirling the pan to coat it with the butter. Add the eggs and asparagus, and gently stir with a silicone spatula to lift the cooked egg off the bottom of the skillet and stir it into the uncooked portion (be careful not to overstir the omelet). As the omelet begins to set, give it one last gentle stir. Then scatter the cheese slices over the top. Place the pan under the broiler and cook for about 1 minute, or until the omelet is set on top and the cheese has melted. Using the silicone spatula, loosen the omelet from the pan, slide it onto a platter, and serve.

portobello mushrooms with ricotta, tomatoes, and basil

If there are vegetarians in your group, you can't go wrong with this pretty, healthful dish. It's robust enough to serve as an entrée, but it also goes very nicely indeed with a few slabs of bacon and a fried or scrambled egg.

Serves 4

3 medium heirloom tomatoes (about 1 pound total), halved and cored

1 cup cherry tomatoes, halved

3 tablespoons extra-virgin olive oil

Salt and freshly ground black pepper

3 or 4 fresh thyme sprigs

4 portobello mushrooms, stems removed

4 ounces (about ½ cup) fresh ricotta cheese

2 tablespoons small fresh basil leaves

Position an oven rack about 8 inches below the heating element and preheat the broiler to low heat. Arrange the tomatoes cut side up on a large heavy baking sheet. Drizzle 1 tablespoon of the olive oil over the tomatoes, and sprinkle with salt, pepper, and the thyme. Broil the tomatoes for 5 to 7 minutes.

Arrange the mushrooms, gill side up, on the same baking sheet with the tomatoes, and drizzle 1 tablespoon of the olive oil over them. Turn the mushrooms over and brush the tops with the remaining 1 tablespoon oil. Broil the mushrooms and tomatoes for 5 minutes.

Turn the mushrooms gill side up, and spoon the ricotta onto the mushrooms. Continue broiling for a further 5 minutes, or until the ricotta is heated through and beginning to brown on top. At this point, the mushrooms and tomatoes should be just tender and the tomatoes should be slightly browned on top. Transfer them to a platter, sprinkle with the basil, and serve.

toasted bagels with crispy prosciutto, poached eggs, and spinach

When you bake prosciutto in the oven, it becomes deliciously crispy and holds a shape. Here I've baked it in muffin cups to make the perfect vessel for poached eggs. It's so simple to do, and yet your guests will think you're a five-star chef!

Serves 8

16 slices prosciutto

¼ cup white wine vinegar

8 large eggs

1 tablespoon (⅛ stick) butter

6 cups (packed) fresh spinach leaves

4 bagels, split and toasted

Preheat the oven to 400°F. Use 2 slices of prosciutto to line each of 8 standard muffin cups (it's best to use 2 muffin pans, each with 12 cups, and space them out so that the prosciutto slices in one cup don't overlap the slices in another cup). Set the muffin pans on large, rimmed baking sheets (to catch any drips) and bake for 18 minutes, or until the prosciutto shrinks, becomes crisp, and forms cups.

Meanwhile, fill a large skillet with water and bring it to a simmer over medium heat. Stir in the vinegar. Crack 1 egg into a coffee cup or a small bowl and then gently transfer the egg to the simmering water. Repeat with 3 more eggs. Cook the eggs for about 3 minutes, or until the whites are set but the yolks are still runny. Using a slotted spoon, carefully remove the eggs from the simmering water and set them on a paper towel to drain the excess water. Repeat with the remaining 4 eggs.

While the second batch of eggs is poaching, melt the butter in a large sauté pan over high heat. Add the spinach and sauté for 2 minutes, or just until the spinach wilts.

Set the toasted bagel halves cut side up on 8 plates. Spoon the wilted spinach atop the bagels, dividing it evenly. Set the prosciutto cups atop the spinach. Spoon the eggs into the prosciutto cups, and serve.

scrambled eggs with smoked salmon and chives

We shouldn't call these eggs "scrambled"; they are more like fluffy curds, and so light you'll feel like you're eating clouds. For a recipe this simple, be sure to use the very best ingredients you can get your hands on. I have the same rule for buying both smoked salmon and eggs: In general, you get what you pay for, so go for the organic eggs and the deli-sliced salmon, not the packaged stuff; it makes a real difference.

Serves 4

6 large eggs

$2/3$ cup heavy cream

$1/4$ cup 1-inch pieces fresh chives

$1/4$ teaspoon salt

$1/4$ teaspoon freshly ground black pepper

2 tablespoons ($1/4$ stick) butter

4 slices sourdough bread

8 tablespoons cream cheese

4 ounces sliced cold-smoked salmon

4 lemon wedges

Using a fork, mix the eggs, cream, chives, salt, and pepper in a large bowl to blend. Melt the butter in a large heavy nonstick skillet over medium-low heat. Add the egg mixture to the skillet and let it cook without stirring for 2 minutes. Once the eggs are just set on the bottom of the skillet, use a silicone spatula to gently push and move the eggs into gentle curds, avoiding breaking them up too much. In all, cook the eggs for about 8 minutes, or until they are no longer runny; don't overstir.

Meanwhile, toast the sourdough bread, and then spread the cream cheese over the toast.

Place a slice of toast, cream cheese side up, on each plate and top with the smoked salmon, dividing it evenly. Spoon the egg mixture over the salmon, and serve with the lemon wedges alongside.

spicy sausage
breakfast burritos

When I first went surfing in Malibu, I saw all the surfers lined up to get their breakfast burritos after a morning on the waves. Those burritos were so delicious that I worked out how to make them for myself. If you've had a strenuous start to the day, this is the perfect protein payback.

Makes 4

2 spicy (Italian or Spanish-style) sausages

6 large eggs

2/3 cup heavy cream

1/4 teaspoon salt

1/4 teaspoon freshly ground black pepper

2 tablespoons (1/4 stick) butter

2 scallions, white and green parts, thinly sliced

1/2 cup coarsely chopped fresh cilantro

1 red jalapeño, finely chopped

Four 10-inch flour tortillas

Hot sauce (such as Cholula)

Preheat the broiler. Place the sausages on a heavy, rimmed baking sheet and broil for 3 minutes on each side, or until they are cooked through and golden brown. Set the sausages aside until they are cool enough to handle; then cut them diagonally into thin slices.

Using a fork, mix the eggs, cream, salt, and pepper in a large bowl to blend. Melt the butter in a large heavy nonstick sauté pan over medium-low heat. Add the egg mixture. Once the eggs are just set on the bottom of the pan, add the sausages, scallions, cilantro, and jalapeño. Stir the egg mixture very slowly with a silicone spatula, scraping from the bottom of the pan, for 3 to 5 minutes, or until the eggs are no longer runny.

Meanwhile, heat a griddle pan over medium-high heat. Cook each tortilla on the griddle for 1 minute on each side, or until warmed and softened.

Divide the egg mixture among the hot tortillas, and wrap the tortillas around the egg mixture to enclose it completely and form a burrito. Serve with your favorite hot sauce.

crispy tortilla with ham, chile, spinach, and fried eggs

Breakfast sandwiches hit the spot, but sometimes all that bread is a bit of carb overkill. This is a nice change of pace from a ham and cheese omelet, with a spicy kick and a lot of crunchy texture.

Serves 4

Four 10-inch flour tortillas

8 thin slices Black Forest ham

3 tablespoons butter

1 small red jalapeño, finely chopped

8 cups (packed) fresh baby spinach leaves

Salt

8 large organic free-range eggs

1⅓ cups (about 5 ounces) shredded white sharp cheddar cheese

Hot sauce (such as Cholula)

Preheat the broiler. Heat a flat griddle pan over medium-high heat. Working with 1 tortilla at a time, cook the tortillas for 2 minutes on each side, or until they are hot and slightly crisp (do not allow the tortillas to become too crisp at this point, since they will continue to crisp under the broiler). Set 2 tortillas on each of 2 large heavy baking sheets. Lay 2 slices of ham, overlapping slightly, on each tortilla.

Melt 1 tablespoon of the butter in a large sauté pan over medium-high heat. Add the jalapeño and stir to coat with the butter. Add the spinach and sauté for 2 minutes, or just until it wilts. Season to taste with salt, squeeze out any excess moisture, and spoon the spinach atop the ham, dividing it equally.

Melt 1 tablespoon of the butter on the griddle pan over medium-high heat. Crack 4 eggs into the pan, spacing them evenly apart, and cook for 2 minutes, or until the whites are set and beginning to brown around the edges. Using a spatula, carefully set 2 eggs atop the spinach on each of 2 tortillas. Repeat with the remaining 1 tablespoon butter and 4 eggs.

Sprinkle the shredded cheese over the eggs, and broil for 1 to 2 minutes, or until the egg whites are set on top and the cheese has melted. Transfer to plates, and serve with the hot sauce.

homemade waffles with apples and ice cream

When you want to go all out for a very special breakfast—Mother's Day, a birthday brunch—this is a ridiculously decadent treat. I promise, though, that if you try ice cream with waffles for breakfast just one time, it won't be the last. Of course, you can substitute the usual whipped cream or butter for the ice cream, but I don't think the results are quite the same.

Serves 4 to 6

Caramelized apples

¾ cup sugar

1 vanilla bean, split lengthwise

½ cup (1 stick) unsalted butter

5 Pink Lady or Fuji apples (about 2 pounds total), cored and cut into 1-inch-wide wedges

¼ cup heavy cream

Waffles

1½ cups all-purpose flour

3 tablespoons sugar

2¼ teaspoons baking powder

¾ teaspoon baking soda

¾ teaspoon salt

1½ cups whole milk

1 large egg

3 tablespoons unsalted butter, melted

1½ pints vanilla ice cream, for serving

To prepare the caramelized apples: Combine the sugar and ¼ cup water in a large heavy skillet and stir over low heat, occasionally brushing down the sides of the skillet with a wet pastry brush, until the sugar dissolves. Scrape in the seeds from the vanilla bean; then add the bean itself to the sugar mixture. Increase the heat and boil without stirring, occasionally brushing down the sides and swirling the pan, until the syrup is a deep amber color, about 8 minutes. Stir in the butter. Add the apples and stir to coat. Cook, stirring occasionally, for 8 to 10 minutes, or until the apples begin to soften and the sauce thickens slightly. Then stir in the cream and simmer for 2 minutes longer. Discard the vanilla bean. Set aside and keep warm.

To make the waffles: Preheat a Belgian waffle iron and preheat the oven to 200°F. Sift the flour, sugar, baking powder, baking soda, and salt into a large bowl. In another large bowl, whisk the milk, egg, and melted butter to blend. Add the milk mixture to the dry ingredients, whisking constantly to prevent lumps.

Ladle about ½ cup of the waffle batter onto each of the 4½-inch square grids. Cover and cook for 5 to 8 minutes, depending on your iron (most new irons have a timer), or until the waffle is golden and crisp on the outside and cooked through. Transfer the waffles to a baking sheet and keep them warm in the oven while cooking the remaining waffles.

Place the hot waffles on plates. Spoon the caramelized apple mixture over the waffles. Set a scoop of ice cream on top, and serve.

exotic fruit salad with
passion fruit granita

Don't be scared of the word *granita*. It's simply a fruit puree with water and sugar. Once the granita is frozen, it resembles snow. It can be made in advance and stored in the freezer for up to a week, tightly covered. If you have trouble finding passion fruit, try substituting two large ripe mangoes, pureed.

Serves 4

¼ cup sugar

1 pound ripe passion fruit, halved

1 tablespoon fresh lemon juice

½ pineapple, peeled, cored, and cut into bite-size pieces (about 4 cups)

1 papaya, peeled, seeded, and cut into bite-size pieces (about 2½ cups)

1 mango, peeled, pitted, and cut into bite-size pieces (about 2 cups)

1 star fruit, cut into ¼-inch-thick slices

4 kiwis, cut into bite-size pieces (about 2 cups)

1 tablespoon chopped fresh mint leaves (optional)

In a small heavy saucepan, stir 1 cup water and the sugar together over medium-low heat until the sugar dissolves. Slowly bring the syrup to a boil; then remove it from the heat and let it cool completely.

Spoon the passion fruit flesh into the cooled syrup and mix together. Stir in the lemon juice. Pour the passion fruit mixture into an 8-inch square baking dish and freeze it for about 30 minutes, or until the mixture is icy around the edges.

Using a large fork, stir the icy parts of the passion fruit mixture into the remaining mixture in the dish. Continue to freeze the mixture, stirring the edges into the center every 20 to 30 minutes, for about 1½ hours longer, or until it is frozen. Using a large fork, scrape the frozen granita into flaky crystals. Cover and keep frozen.

In a large bowl, gently toss the pineapple, papaya, mango, star fruit, and chopped mint, if using. Spoon the mixed fruit into serving bowls, and top each one with a large spoonful of granita. Garnish with the mint sprigs, and serve.

chapter three
weekend lunches

In some ways, I really prefer lunch to dinner—especially on the weekend. There's no pressure to move on. The whole day is ahead of you, and you can eat at as leisurely a pace as you like.

I love to kick off the weekend with a trip to my local farmer's market to restock my pantry and fridge. There's nothing more inspiring than wandering around the market, getting ideas about what I'd like to cook (you can usually also get something to eat right there, which makes it even better). It puts me in a good mood, talking to the people who produce the food, sharing their knowledge about their products. I feed off their pride, and I always learn something.

Once my kitchen is filled with the results of my shopping trip, what better way to catch up with friends and family than sitting around the dining table? I find that making light food that's incredibly tasty and serving it in the middle of the day sets the stage for great conversation and allows us time to linger. I love tasty soups, yummy tarts, and show-stopping salads that leave friends begging for an invite back next weekend—and that won't make them feel like they need to sleep off a huge meal.

Of course, these dishes could also be served as a light supper or could play a part in a bigger spread. So relax; phone some special people and invite them over this weekend. I promise you'll have fun.

chilled gazpacho

A diced cucumber garnish gives this smooth, pureed soup a nice texture, and the drizzle of olive oil gives it a bit more richness. For some fun, serve it in shot glasses before lunch or at a party.

Serves 6

2 pounds ripe tomatoes
(about 6), coarsely chopped

1 cup chicken stock

1 cup reduced-sodium 100%
organic vegetable juice cocktail

1/3 cup red wine vinegar

1/2 cucumber, peeled, seeded,
and coarsely chopped

1/2 red bell pepper, seeded and
coarsely chopped

One 5-inch piece of baguette,
crust removed

1 shallot, coarsely chopped

1 garlic clove, bruised

1/2 teaspoon ground coriander

1/2 teaspoon ground cumin

Salt and freshly ground black
pepper

1/2 cup finely diced seeded
peeled cucumber, for garnish

3 tablespoons extra-virgin
olive oil

Combine all the soup ingredients in a large bowl.
Cover and refrigerate for 12 hours.

Transfer the soup ingredients to a food processor or blender, and blitz until smooth. Refrigerate the soup until it is very cold. Season with more salt and pepper if needed.

Ladle the chilled soup into chilled bowls, and garnish with the finely diced cucumbers. Drizzle with the extra-virgin olive oil, and serve.

roasted fennel and
potato soup

If you have never tried fennel soup, you are really missing out on something unique. It's like a leek and potato soup with a bit more interest and a great silky texture that just begs for a roaring fire on a wintry day. By roasting the fennel you achieve a lovely charred flavor throughout the soup.

Serves 6

2 fennel bulbs, trimmed and coarsely chopped

1 small onion, coarsely chopped

2 tablespoons olive oil

2 garlic cloves

1 leek (white and pale green parts only), coarsely chopped

6 cups chicken stock

1 pound russet potatoes, peeled and cut into large chunks

1 cup heavy cream

Salt and freshly ground black pepper

1 bunch fresh chives, chopped (¼ cup)

Preheat the oven to 350°F. Toss the fennel and onions with 1 tablespoon of the oil on a large heavy baking sheet, coating the vegetables. Roast in the oven, stirring occasionally, for 25 minutes, or until the fennel and onions are tender. Set aside.

Heat the remaining 1 tablespoon oil in a large heavy saucepan over medium heat. Add the garlic and sauté for 1 minute. Add the leeks and sauté for 5 minutes, or until they have softened slightly. Add the stock, potatoes, and roasted fennel mixture, and bring to a simmer. Continue simmering for 18 minutes, or until the potatoes are very tender. Remove the soup from the heat and let it cool slightly.

Working in batches, puree the soup in a blender until smooth. Strain the soup into a clean large saucepan. Add the cream to the soup and bring to a simmer over medium-high heat, stirring occasionally. Season with salt and pepper to taste. Ladle the soup into bowls, garnish with the chives, and serve.

classic french onion soup

Sometimes classics are meant to be served simply, and this is one such example. The light soup, the rich onion flavor, and the soothing quality of the melty cheese *croûte* are really all you need for a perfect bowl of soup. This soup can be made a couple of days in advance, and it also freezes well; reheat and then top with the cheese croutons.

Serves 6

2 tablespoons olive oil

6 onions (about 3 pounds total), thinly sliced

4 garlic cloves, finely chopped

2 large sprigs fresh thyme

1 bay leaf

½ cup dry red wine

½ cup dry sherry

8 cups good-quality beef stock

Salt and freshly ground black pepper

Six ¾-inch-thick slices sourdough bread

6 ounces Gruyère cheese, shredded

2 tablespoons thinly sliced fresh flat-leaf parsley

Place a large heavy pot over medium heat. Drizzle the oil into the hot pot and add the onions. Cook, stirring often, for 40 minutes, or until the onions are golden. (Once the onions become very soft, they will begin to stick to the bottom of the pot and turn a caramel-brown color. As this occurs, scrape the browned onions from the bottom of the pot and stir them into the remaining onion mixture.)

Add the garlic, thyme, and bay leaf to the onions and cook for 5 minutes, or until the garlic softens. Then add the red wine and sherry, and stir to scrape up any browned bits on the bottom of the pan. Simmer for 5 minutes, or until the liquid has reduced by half. Add the stock and bring the soup to a gentle simmer, skimming off any foam that rises to the top. Allow the soup to simmer, uncovered, for 25 minutes. Season the soup with salt and pepper to taste.

Preheat the broiler. Arrange the bread slices on a baking sheet and broil for 2 minutes or until golden brown. Turn the slices over and generously sprinkle the cheese and parsley over the untoasted side. Return to the broiler for 3 minutes, or until the cheese melts and is golden brown.

Place a cheesy crouton on top of each bowl of soup, and serve.

seafood wonton soup

Wontons are simple and fun to make, and every time I've made them with kids, they go crazy for the soup, which is full of goodness.

Serves 4

Wontons

2 jumbo scallops

1 large egg yolk

4 ounces shrimp, peeled, deveined, and coarsely chopped

1 Napa cabbage leaf, finely chopped

1 tablespoon light soy sauce

1 teaspoon Shaoxing rice wine (yellow rice wine)

1/4 teaspoon toasted sesame oil

1 tablespoon oyster sauce

1 small garlic clove, finely chopped

Cornstarch, for dusting

24 wonton wrappers (see Note)

Soup

6 cups fish stock or chicken stock

2 tablespoons light soy sauce

2 tablespoons Shaoxing rice wine (yellow rice wine)

1/2 teaspoon toasted sesame oil

4 baby bok choy, cut lengthwise into thin strips

To make the wontons: Place the scallops in a food processor and puree to make a paste. Blend in half of the egg yolk (discard the remaining yolk). Transfer the scallop puree to a medium bowl. Stir in the shrimp, cabbage, soy sauce, rice wine, sesame oil, oyster sauce, and garlic.

Lightly dust a baking sheet with cornstarch. Place 1 wonton wrapper on a flat surface and place a generous teaspoon of the shrimp mixture in the center. Lightly brush the edges of the wrapper with a little water. Fold the wrapper in half, pressing the edges to seal them and forming a rectangular-shaped dumpling. Moisten two folded corners with water, bring the corners together, and press them firmly to adhere. Place the wonton on the prepared baking sheet. Repeat with the remaining wrappers and shrimp mixture.

To make the soup: Place the stock in a medium pot and bring it to a boil over high heat. Add the soy sauce, rice wine, and sesame oil to the stock. Reduce the heat to a rolling simmer and add the seafood wontons. Cook for approximately 4 minutes, or until the filling is cooked through. Then add the bok choy to the soup and cook for 1 minute, until it wilts. Ladle the soup into 4 serving bowls, dividing the bok choy and wontons evenly, and serve.

Note
Whether you find wonton skins or dumpling wrappers, the results will be very similar. Practice sealing them in different ways to find your favorite shape.

scallop ceviche with
chile pepper, lime, and soy

Scallop ceviche is so simple to prepare because no cooking is required. For something different, I've incorporated Asian flavors into this classic South American preparation. The two cuisines have a lot in common because they are designed to cool the palate in torrid temperatures, combining bright, fresh flavors like chile and citrus with crisp textures. You can substitute light brown sugar for the palm sugar if you like.

Serves 4

½ cup vegetable oil, for frying

6 garlic cloves

2 shallots

⅓ cup fresh lime juice

1 jalapeño, finely chopped

1 tablespoon unsweetened coconut milk

1 tablespoon light soy sauce

1 (packed) tablespoon grated palm sugar (jaggery)

2 drops toasted sesame oil

8 large sea scallops, each cut horizontally into 4 thin rounds

2 small firm but ripe avocados, pitted, peeled, and cubed

2 tablespoons small fresh basil leaves, coarsely chopped

2 tablespoons small fresh mint leaves, coarsely chopped

Heat the vegetable oil in a wok or skillet over medium heat. Using a mandoline or a very sharp knife, very thinly slice the garlic and shallots. Add the garlic to the hot oil and fry for 1 minute, or until crisp and golden. Using a mesh skimmer or a slotted spoon, transfer the fried garlic to paper towels to absorb the excess oil. Repeat with the shallots.

Stir the lime juice, jalapeño, coconut milk, soy sauce, palm sugar, and sesame oil in a large bowl to combine. Add the scallops and let stand, tossing them occasionally, for 15 minutes, or until the lime juice begins to "cook" the outer surfaces of the scallops and they become whiter and opaque.

Using a slotted spoon, remove the scallop slices from the marinade and arrange them, overlapping slightly, in the center of 4 serving plates, dividing them equally. Top with the avocado, basil, and mint. Drizzle with the marinade. Sprinkle with the fried garlic and shallots, and serve.

lobster cocktail

We all love shrimp cocktail, and for good reason—it's just a great way to start a meal. This is a glammed-up version of the old classic, and if you are looking to impress, you could upgrade it even further to a mixture of shrimp, crab, and lobster. In the U.K. and Australia we always put mayonnaise in our cocktail sauce, which gives it a richer flavor than the typical American tomato-based staple. I add a bit of crème fraîche to smooth it out.

Serves 4

Two 2- to 2½-pound live lobsters

¼ cup crème fraîche

¼ cup organic mayonnaise

2 tablespoons ketchup

2 teaspoons prepared horseradish

1½ tablespoons fresh lemon juice

Salt and freshly ground black pepper

2½ tablespoons finely chopped fresh chives

¼ head iceberg lettuce, very thinly shredded

Lemon wedges, for garnish

Place the lobsters in the freezer for 30 minutes so they become sleepy. Meanwhile, bring a very large pot of water to a boil over high heat.

Working with one at a time, add the lobsters to the boiling water and cook for 7 minutes. Using tongs, transfer the lobsters to a large bowl. Cover the bowl with plastic wrap and set it aside for 2 minutes. Then remove the plastic wrap and set the bowl aside for 10 minutes, or until the lobsters are cool enough to handle. Cut off the tails and claws, and crack them to extract the meat, using sharp scissors or poultry shears to cut through the shells. Cut the tail meat and claw meat into bite-size pieces. Transfer the lobster meat to a bowl, cover, and refrigerate until cold.

Stir the crème fraîche, mayonnaise, ketchup, and horse-radish in a medium bowl to blend; then mix in the lemon juice. Season the sauce to taste with a little salt and pepper. Toss the lobster pieces with the sauce and 2 tablespoons of the chives. Divide the lettuce among 4 martini-type glasses. Spoon the lobster mixture over the lettuce, and sprinkle with the remaining chives. Garnish with the lemon wedges, and serve.

onion tarts with taleggio cheese

A savory version of tarte Tatin is one of the most beautiful things you can serve, and it is surprisingly easy to make. These upside-down tarts can be made well in advance; simply heat them up before you serve them. Delicious and so very indulgent.

The directions below are for making individual tarts. If you don't have four small pans you can simply make one larger tart in a ten-inch skillet and cut it in wedges to serve.

Serves 4

8 tablespoons (1 stick) unsalted butter, room temperature

12 tablespoons sugar

1 very large onion, peeled

1 sheet frozen puff pastry, thawed (see Note)

½ cup balsamic vinegar

4 ounces Taleggio cheese, cut into 4 slices

Note

Most commercial puff pastry is made with margarine as opposed to pure butter. If you are able to find all-butter puff pastry, buy it—it has a rich buttery flavor instead of a chemical taste.

Spread 2 tablespoons of the butter over the bottom of each of 4 small heavy ovenproof sauté pans. Sprinkle 3 table-spoons of the sugar over the butter in each small pan. Cut the onion crosswise into four 1-inch-thick slices, keeping the rings intact. Place 1 onion slice atop the sugar and butter in each small pan. Refrigerate while you prepare the pastry.

Unfold the puff pastry sheet and roll it out on a lightly floured work surface to form a 12-inch square. Cut out four 5-inch rounds from the puff pastry sheet. Drape 1 pastry round over each onion slice, and tuck the edges down to cover the onion. Pierce the tops of the pastry rounds with a sharp knife, and refrigerate for 20 minutes.

Meanwhile, preheat the oven to 375°F. Simmer the balsamic vinegar in a small heavy saucepan over medium heat for 10 minutes, or until it is reduced by half and coats the back of a spoon. Set it aside to cool. The balsamic reduction will continue to thicken and become syrupy as it cools.

Place the sauté pans over medium heat and cook for 5 minutes, or just until the sugar melts and forms a very pale golden caramel sauce around the tart. Transfer the pans to the oven and bake for about 15 minutes, or until the puff pastry is golden brown and the sauce has darkened.

Let the tarts stand for 2 minutes, or until the sauce stops bubbling. Swirl the tarts gently to help loosen the onions from the bottom of the pans. Invert each tart onto a plate, using a metal spatula if necessary. Immediately place 1 slice of cheese atop each hot tart. Drizzle the balsamic reduction around the tarts, and serve.

wild mushroom, spinach, and goat cheese tarts

The thing I love about tarts is that you can fill them as the season and your taste dictate. In the fall I love packing them full of wild mushrooms. When the season changes, substitute your favorite vegetables, from asparagus to tomato and red onion.

Serves 4

Crust

¾ cup all-purpose flour

4 tablespoons (½ stick) chilled unsalted butter, cut into pieces

¼ teaspoon salt

3 tablespoons ice-cold water

Filling

1 tablespoon olive oil

8 ounces assorted wild mushrooms, trimmed and cut into bite-size pieces

1 shallot, coarsely chopped

2 cups (tightly packed) fresh baby spinach leaves

2 ounces soft fresh goat cheese, coarsely crumbled

½ cup heavy cream

2 large eggs

½ teaspoon salt

¼ teaspoon freshly ground black pepper

To make the crust: Combine the flour, butter, and salt in a food processor and blend until the mixture resembles breadcrumbs. Add the ice-cold water and continue to blend until moist clumps begin to form. Transfer the dough to a work surface, pat it into a ball, and cut the ball into 4 pieces. Flatten each piece into a disk shape, and wrap in plastic wrap. Refrigerate for 1 hour, or until the disks are semi-firm.

Lightly coat four 4½-inch-diameter tart pans with removable bottoms with butter. Unwrap the dough disks and roll each one out on a lightly floured work surface to form a ¼-inch-thick round. Transfer the dough to the prepared tart pans; fold the overhang in and press it gently to adhere. Refrigerate for 30 minutes, or until the pastry shells are firm.

Meanwhile, preheat the oven to 400°F. Line the pastry shells with foil and weight the foil down with pie weights or dried beans. Place the tart pans on a baking sheet and bake for 15 minutes. Remove the weights and foil and continue baking for 8 minutes, or until the crusts are pale gold.

Meanwhile, prepare the filling: Heat the oil in a large heavy sauté pan over medium-high heat. Add the mushrooms and shallots and sauté for 3 minutes, or until the mushrooms soften. Add the spinach and sauté for 1 minute, or just until the spinach wilts. Remove the pan from the heat. When the spinach mixture is cool, drain off the excess moisture.

Divide the spinach-mushroom mixture among the 4 warm crusts. Top with the crumbled cheese. Mix the cream, eggs, salt, and pepper in a medium bowl to blend. Pour the egg mixture over the filling. Bake for 18 minutes, or until the custard is just set in the center. Let the tarts cool for 5 minutes. Then remove them from the pans, and serve.

cheesy crêpes with prosciutto, sun-dried tomatoes, and olives

The thing about crêpes is that they're just a vehicle for delivering wonderful flavors. The fillings are up to you—they can be as fancy as this or as simple as cheese and ham or Nutella and sliced bananas. If you're having lots of people around for lunch, serving crêpes is a good way to let everyone cater to their own dietary needs and preferences. Kids enjoy making them, too. I love hosting crêpe nights, offering an array of fillings that swing from savory to sweet.

Serves 4

Crêpes

1¼ cups whole milk

1 cup all-purpose flour, sifted

½ cup heavy cream

2 large eggs

4 teaspoons sugar

Pinch of salt

1 tablespoon (⅛ stick) unsalted butter

14 ounces white cheddar cheese, grated

2 ounces feta cheese, crumbled

¾ cup oil-packed sun-dried tomatoes, drained of excess oil and thinly sliced

½ cup kalamata olives, pitted and sliced

6 thin slices prosciutto, torn into bite-size pieces

To make the crêpes: Blend the milk, flour, cream, eggs, sugar, and salt in a blender until smooth. Transfer the batter to a medium bowl, cover, and set aside for 30 minutes.

Preheat the oven to 200°F. Heat a heavy 8-inch nonstick sauté pan over medium-low heat. Dab some of the butter on a paper towel and wipe the pan with it. Pour 3 tablespoons of the batter into the center of the pan and swirl to coat the bottom thinly. Cook until the edge of the crêpe is light brown, about 1½ minutes. Loosen the edges gently with a spatula, and carefully turn the crêpe over. Sprinkle a little of the cheddar, then a little of the feta, sun-dried tomatoes, olives, and prosciutto, over half of the crêpe. Cook until the bottom begins to brown in spots and the cheese melts, about 1 minute. Fold the uncovered side of the crêpe over the filling. Transfer to a baking sheet and tent with foil. Place in the oven to keep warm while you make the remaining crêpes. Repeat with the remaining batter and fillings, wiping the pan with butter as needed and forming 8 crêpes total.

Salad

¼ cup extra-virgin olive oil

3 tablespoons red wine vinegar

Salt and freshly ground black pepper

4 cups fresh arugula leaves

¼ English cucumber, peeled, halved lengthwise, then thinly sliced crosswise

8 cherry tomatoes, halved

2 tablespoons thinly sliced fresh basil

To prepare the salad: Whisk the oil and vinegar in a medium bowl to blend, and season the vinaigrette with salt and pepper to taste. Toss the arugula, cucumber, tomatoes, and basil in a large bowl with enough vinaigrette to coat. Season the salad with freshly ground pepper to taste.

Mound the salad on each of 4 plates. Place 2 folded crêpes on each plate alongside the salad. Drizzle the remaining vinaigrette over and around the crêpes, and serve.

simple salad with parmesan wafers
and organic poached egg

It's the texture of the crunchy fresh leaves that really tells your body that you are being good to it. Combine that with crisp Parmesan wafers and warm gooey poached egg, and your taste buds will thank you as well.

Serves 4

2 large organic egg yolks

1 tablespoon Dijon mustard

1 large garlic clove

$1/3$ cup plus 2 tablespoons white wine vinegar

$1/2$ cup grated Parmesan cheese

$1/2$ cup grapeseed oil

Salt and freshly ground black pepper

$3/4$ cup shredded Parmesan cheese

4 large organic eggs

1 head romaine lettuce, coarsely chopped

1 head butter lettuce, coarsely chopped

$1/4$ bunch fresh flat-leaf parsley, coarsely chopped (about $1/2$ cup)

Preheat the oven to 400°F. Combine the egg yolks, mustard, and garlic in a blender and blend until the garlic is minced. Blend in $1/3$ cup vinegar, then the grated Parmesan cheese. With the machine running, slowly add the oil in a thin, constant stream until the dressing is nice and creamy. Season the dressing with salt and pepper to taste. Remove the dressing from the blender and reserve.

Place a nonstick silicone mat or a sheet of parchment paper on a large baking sheet. Evenly sprinkle the shredded Parmesan cheese over the mat, forming a thin 13 x 9-inch rectangle of cheese. Bake for about 7 minutes, or until the cheese is lacy and golden. Remove from the oven and allow to cool completely. Then break the Parmesan wafer into large pieces.

Bring a large skillet of water to a simmer over high heat. Stir the water and add the remaining 2 tablespoons vinegar. Crack 1 egg into a small bowl and then gently transfer the egg to the simmering water. Repeat with the remaining 3 eggs. Allow the eggs to poach for about 3 minutes, or until the whites are set but the yolks are still runny. Using a slotted spoon, gently remove the eggs from the simmering water and set them on a paper towel to absorb the excess water.

Toss the romaine lettuce, butter lettuce, and parsley in a large bowl with enough dressing to coat. Season the salad with salt and pepper to taste.

Divide the salad among 4 serving bowls. Place the Parmesan wafers over the salad and top each salad with a poached egg. Sprinkle the eggs with black pepper, and serve.

heirloom tomato and burrata salad
with pepper-crusted new york steak

This salad is full of protein and iron, so if you will be hitting the gym, it is great fuel. Burrata is a cow's-milk version of mozzarella that is so creamy it's almost spreadable. If I have any salad left over, I turn it into a filling for a panino the next day.

Serves 4

2 tablespoons whole black peppercorns, coarsely crushed

Four 8-ounce New York strip steaks

Sea salt

4 teaspoons plus 3 tablespoons extra-virgin olive oil

3 tablespoons balsamic vinegar

Salt and freshly ground black pepper

6 medium heirloom tomatoes, halved and cored

8 ounces fresh baby spinach leaves or mixed baby greens

1 small red onion, thinly sliced

1 ball fresh burrata, torn into pieces

Heat a barbecue grill to medium-high. Place the coarsely crushed peppercorns on a plate. Press both sides of the steaks into the peppercorns, coating the steaks. Sprinkle the steaks with sea salt to taste, and drizzle 1 teaspoon of the olive oil over each steak.

Whisk the vinegar and the 3 tablespoons olive oil in a medium bowl to blend, and season the vinaigrette with salt and pepper to taste. Place the heirloom tomatoes in a large bowl, and add the baby spinach leaves and red onions. Toss the salad with the vinaigrette.

Grill the steaks, oiled side down first, for about 4 minutes on each side for medium-rare. Remove the steaks from the grill and let them rest for 5 minutes. Using a large sharp knife, cut the steaks across the grain into thin slices.

Divide the salad among 4 serving plates. Arrange the slices of steak on top of the salad, and surround the salad with the pieces of cheese. Serve immediately.

arugula salad with pomegranate, persimmon, and toasted hazelnuts

This truly is a magical salad, popping with color and goodness. Pomegranates are full of antioxidants and vitamins, making this tasty dish a tribute to the healing powers of Mother Nature.

Serves 4

⅓ cup hazelnuts

5 ounces baby arugula leaves

½ cup pomegranate seeds (from 1 pomegranate)

1 firm but ripe Fuyu (flat-bottomed) persimmon, cut into thin wedges

3 tablespoons raspberry vinegar

2 tablespoons pomegranate juice

¼ cup grapeseed oil

3 tablespoons extra-virgin olive oil

Salt and freshly ground black pepper

Preheat the oven to 350°F. Place the hazelnuts on a baking sheet and toast in the oven, shaking the pan occasionally to ensure that they brown evenly, for about 8 minutes. Remove from the oven and set aside to cool. Rub the cooled hazelnuts between your palms to loosen the brown husks, allowing the husks to fall to the work surface. Discard the husks and coarsely chop the hazelnuts.

Combine the arugula leaves with the pomegranate seeds and persimmon wedges in a large mixing bowl.

In a separate mixing bowl, whisk together the raspberry vinegar and pomegranate juice. Slowly add the grapeseed oil and the olive oil while whisking constantly to blend. Season the vinaigrette with salt and pepper to taste.

Gently toss the salad with enough vinaigrette to coat, and season to taste with salt and pepper. Mound the salad onto 4 plates. Sprinkle any pomegranate seeds that have fallen to the bottom of the bowl over the salads. Sprinkle with the toasted hazelnuts, and serve.

baby spinach salad with crispy bacon and cheese croutons

Think of this as a BLT on a health kick. If you are into strong-flavored cheese, you may like to substitute Parmesan for the Dry Jack. If you're cooking for other people, bacon is always a sure winner—the second they walk in the door they'll be hungry from that great smell.

Serves 4

4 thick slices crusty sourdough bread

4 tablespoons (½ stick) butter

1 ounce Dry Jack cheese, finely shredded

3 tablespoons red wine vinegar

6 tablespoons grapeseed oil

1 tablespoon coarsely chopped fresh flat-leaf parsley

Salt and freshly ground black pepper

8 slices bacon

8 cups fresh baby spinach leaves

12 cherry tomatoes, halved

Preheat the oven to 400°F. Using a serrated knife, remove the crusts from the sourdough bread. Then tear or cut the bread into 1-inch pieces. Place the bread pieces on a baking sheet and toast in the oven, stirring the pieces halfway through to ensure they cook evenly, for 8 minutes or until they are dry and crisp. Remove from the oven but leave the oven on.

Melt the butter in a small saucepan, and drizzle it over the croutons; toss to coat them with the butter. Arrange the butter-coated croutons close together in a single layer on the baking sheet. Sprinkle the cheese generously over the croutons and return them to the oven. Bake for about 5 minutes, or until the cheese has melted and the croutons are golden. Remove the croutons from the oven and set them aside to cool.

Place the vinegar in a medium bowl. Slowly add the oil while whisking constantly to blend. Whisk in the parsley, and season the vinaigrette with salt and pepper to taste.

Preheat a large frying pan over medium heat. Add the bacon and cook for about 3 minutes per side, or until crisp and golden. Transfer the bacon to paper towels to drain.

Meanwhile, in a large bowl, toss the spinach leaves with enough vinaigrette to coat, and season with salt and pepper to taste.

Break half the bacon into bite-size pieces and add them to the salad. Divide the salad among 4 serving plates, and arrange the remaining bacon over the salads. Garnish the salads with the cherry tomatoes and the croutons, and serve.

sashimi salad with soy and orange

Super-healthy and really light, this beautiful salad is bright-looking and -tasting. These days it's not too difficult to find great-quality raw salmon. If you ask your local market for sushi-grade salmon, its freshness will be guaranteed. Once you have found the salmon, the hard work is done.

Serves 4

4 oranges

1 or 2 limes

1 tablespoon soy sauce

3 tablespoons grapeseed oil

6 cups mâche (lamb's lettuce) leaves

2 cups frisée lettuce, torn into bite-size pieces

½ cucumber, peeled, seeded, and thinly sliced (optional)

7 ounces sushi-grade salmon, skin removed

1 teaspoon sesame seeds, toasted

Grate the zest of 1 orange and 1 lime into a large bowl. Squeeze 1 tablespoon of juice from the grated orange and 2 tablespoons of juice from the grated lime into the bowl (you may need a second lime to get the 2 tablespoons of juice). Whisk in the soy sauce and the oil. Set the dressing aside.

Use a sharp knife to slice the rind and pith from the remaining oranges. Working over a large mixing bowl, cut between the membranes to free the orange segments, letting them drop into the bowl. Pour any juice into a cup and reserve it for another use. Add the mâche, frisée, and cucumbers, if using, to the orange segments. Using a large sharp knife, cut the salmon into ⅓-inch-thick slices. Add the salmon to the bowl. Drizzle with the dressing, and toss gently to coat. Allow the flavors to meld for at least 2 minutes.

Divide the salad among 4 serving plates. Sprinkle with the toasted sesame seeds, and serve.

pan-fried calamari with roasted asparagus salad

The combination of asparagus and calamari is unusual, but trust me, it really works. It's so important to get your hands on calamari that is very fresh. The size of the calamari can vary, but the freshness cannot. So go make friends with the fish guy; it will pay off.

Serves 4

Grated zest and juice of 2 limes

1 shallot, finely chopped

1 small serrano chile, seeded and finely chopped

3 tablespoons plus 2 teaspoons extra-virgin olive oil

8 ounces cleaned baby squid (calamari) tubes and tentacles

Sea salt

16 asparagus spears, trimmed and cut into 2-inch pieces

Freshly ground black pepper

2 tablespoons peanut oil

4 ounces mixed baby lettuce leaves

In a medium mixing bowl, combine the lime zest, shallots, serrano chile, and 1 tablespoon of the olive oil, and mix together. Cut the calamari tubes in half lengthwise, and then score the pieces lightly in a diamond pattern. Add the calamari pieces and tentacles to the lime zest mixture, and toss thoroughly to coat. Season the calamari mixture with sea salt. Cover and refrigerate for 1 hour.

Preheat the oven to 375°F. Place the asparagus pieces on a small baking sheet and drizzle with the 2 teaspoons olive oil. Sprinkle with sea salt and pepper. Roast the asparagus for about 8 minutes, or until tender.

Meanwhile, place 2 tablespoons of the lime juice in another medium bowl. While whisking, slowly add the peanut oil and the remaining 2 tablespoons olive oil to blend well. Season the vinaigrette with sea salt and pepper to taste.

Heat a large heavy sauté pan over high heat. Add the calamari mixture to the hot pan and sauté for about 2 minutes, or just until the calamari becomes opaque. Do not overcook the calamari or it will become tough.

Mound the lettuce leaves on 4 plates. Arrange the hot calamari and roasted asparagus over the lettuce. Drizzle some of the vinaigrette over the salads, and serve.

crab and mozzarella salad with
mint and lemon dressing

You might not think to mix crab with cheese, but mozzarella is so mild that it won't overpower the beautiful crabmeat, and it's a great vehicle for flavors. Crab is one of my favorite foods in the world and it needs to be treated with respect. When you're serving really fresh seafood (which is the only kind you should buy), you should always serve it with something crunchy and refreshing, just like these salad leaves. Make sure you get your hands on buffalo mozzarella (cheese made from buffalo milk). It should be sold and stored in a little of the mozzarella water to ensure freshness and maintain its soft texture.

Serves 4

3 tablespoons fresh lemon juice

1/3 cup extra-virgin olive oil

8 ounces Alaskan king crab meat (white meat only)

1 tablespoon thinly sliced fresh chives

5 fresh mint leaves, thinly sliced

Salt and freshly ground black pepper

1 bunch frisée lettuce, outer wilted leaves discarded, remaining leaves separated

One 7- to 8-ounce ball fresh buffalo mozzarella cheese

Place the lemon juice in a medium bowl. Slowly add the olive oil, whisking constantly until the dressing is nice and creamy. Combine the crabmeat, chives, mint, and half of the dressing (about 1/4 cup) in another medium bowl, and toss to coat. Season the crab mixture with salt and pepper to taste.

Divide the lettuce evenly among 4 plates. Tear the mozzarella into large bite-size pieces and scatter the cheese atop the lettuce. Spoon the crab mixture over the salad. Drizzle the plates with the remaining dressing, and serve.

greek salad with char-grilled salmon

A good Greek salad can hardly be improved upon—it is full of strong flavors yet it somehow still comes off as very fresh and light. I was trying to work out how I could serve one as an entrée, and this is spot on. See the photograph on page 63.

Serves 4

Salmon

Eight 2-ounce skinless salmon fillets

Salt and freshly ground black pepper

2 teaspoons garlic-infused extra-virgin olive oil

1 teaspoon dried oregano

Extra-virgin olive oil, for brushing grill

Salad

3 tablespoons red wine vinegar

¼ cup extra-virgin olive oil

Salt and freshly ground black pepper

1 head romaine lettuce, torn into pieces

3 or 4 small heirloom tomatoes, cut into wedges

1 cucumber, peeled, halved lengthwise, seeded, and sliced crosswise

½ cup pitted kalamata olives

½ small red onion, very thinly sliced

4 ounces feta cheese

1 tablespoon chopped fresh flat-leaf parsley

To make the salmon: Prepare a barbecue grill for medium-high heat. Sprinkle the salmon with salt and pepper. Rub the garlic oil and the oregano over the salmon. Brush the hot grill with olive oil. Place the salmon on the oiled grill and cook for 2 minutes on each side, or until it is just cooked through and pale pink in the center.

Meanwhile, prepare the salad: Place the red wine vinegar in a large bowl. Slowly add the olive oil, whisking constantly to blend. Season the vinaigrette with salt and pepper to taste. In a large salad bowl, toss the lettuce, tomatoes, cucumbers, olives, and onions with enough vinaigrette to coat. Season the salad with salt and pepper to taste.

Divide the salad among 4 plates. Crumble the feta cheese over the salads. Top each salad with 2 grilled salmon fillets, and sprinkle with the parsley. Drizzle some of the remaining vinaigrette over the salmon, and serve immediately.

shrimp salad with fennel and blood orange

This is a good example of a great, light, nutritious meal you can make even in the middle of winter, when fresh produce is harder to come by. Raw fennel makes this salad really crunchy, and the blood orange juice tints everything a lovely color.

Serves 4

6 blood oranges

½ head butter lettuce, torn into bite-size pieces

½ head oak-leaf or red-leaf lettuce, torn into bite-size pieces

1 small fennel bulb, trimmed and very thinly sliced

2 teaspoons olive oil

20 jumbo shrimp, peeled and deveined but with tails intact

8 tablespoons (1 stick) unsalted butter

2 teaspoons extra-fine capers, drained

2 sprigs fresh tarragon, leaves only, finely chopped

Salt and freshly ground black pepper

Using a sharp knife, slice the peel and white pith from the oranges. Working over a large bowl to catch the juices and using a small sharp knife, cut between the membranes to release the orange segments into the bowl. Transfer the segments to another large bowl. Squeeze enough juice from the segmented oranges into the bowl of accumulated juices to equal ¼ cup total. Set the juice aside.

Add the lettuce leaves and fennel slices to the orange segments, and toss gently to combine. Divide the salad among 4 serving plates.

Heat the oil in a large heavy sauté pan over medium-high heat. Add the shrimp and cook for 2 minutes, or until they start to turn pink. Add the butter and cook for 2 minutes, or until the butter browns and the shrimp are just cooked through. Using tongs, arrange the shrimp atop the salads. Stir the capers, tarragon, and reserved ¼ cup orange juice into the browned butter in the sauté pan, and season the sauce with salt and pepper to taste. Pour the sauce over the salads, and serve.

sesame chicken salad
with mango and cherry tomatoes

It's interesting to use fruit in a salad because it can bring contrast to the dish. Here sesame gives the chicken a rich, toasty flavor, which plays off the sweetness of the mango for a substantial salad and an amazing mix of colors. Fresh raspberries give the vinaigrette a lovely natural sweetness that enhances the flavors of the chicken and sesame.

Serves 4

¼ cup fresh raspberries

¼ cup raspberry vinegar

5 tablespoons grapeseed oil

1 tablespoon extra-virgin olive oil

2 tablespoons thinly sliced fresh chives

Salt and freshly ground black pepper

Twelve 2-ounce chicken tenders

⅔ cup sesame seeds, preferably a mix of black and white

5 ounces fresh baby spinach leaves

10 cherry tomatoes, halved

1 large ripe mango (about 1¼ pounds), peeled, seeded, and cut into bite-size cubes

Using a whisk, mash the raspberries with the vinegar in a medium bowl. Slowly add 3 tablespoons of the grapeseed oil and the extra-virgin olive oil, whisking constantly until the mixture is well blended. Mix in the chives, and season the vinaigrette with salt and pepper to taste.

Season the chicken tenders with salt and pepper, and coat them with the sesame seeds. Heat 1 tablespoon of the grapeseed oil in a large nonstick sauté pan over medium-high heat. Add half of the sesame-coated chicken tenders and cook for about 2 minutes on each side, or until just cooked through and golden brown. Transfer the chicken to paper towels to drain any excess oil. Repeat with the remaining 1 tablespoon grapeseed oil and chicken tenders.

Toss the spinach leaves, tomatoes, and mango together in a large bowl with enough vinaigrette to coat. Season the salad with salt and pepper to taste. Divide the salad among 4 large serving plates. Cut each chicken tender on the diagonal into 4 slices. Arrange the chicken slices over the salads, drizzle with more dressing, and serve.

grilled scallops with fava beans and roasted tomatoes

The beauty of this dish is its utter simplicity. All three flavors are distinctive but still quite delicate. Don't buy scallops that are sitting in a puddle of water; it's a sure sign they've been frozen or chemically treated to retain moisture. A good hot pan is especially important—the scallops will turn a lovely golden color and caramelize without losing any natural juice or flavor.

Serves 4

12 ounces cherry tomatoes

2 tablespoons plus ¼ cup extra-virgin olive oil

Salt and freshly ground black pepper

1¼ pounds fresh fava bean pods, shelled

3 tablespoons champagne vinegar

2 tablespoons finely chopped fresh mint leaves

12 jumbo sea scallops

Preheat the oven to 400°F. Place the tomatoes in a small baking dish. Drizzle 1 tablespoon of the olive oil over the tomatoes and gently jostle them to coat them with the oil. Sprinkle with salt and pepper. Roast the tomatoes in the oven for 15 minutes, or until they are heated through and just beginning to split. Set the tomatoes aside to cool slightly.

Bring a medium saucepan of salted water to a boil, add the fava beans, and cook for 1 to 2 minutes. Then drain, and transfer the beans to a bowl of ice water to cool. Peel the cooled beans and set them aside.

Whisk the vinegar and the ¼ cup extra-virgin olive oil in a large bowl to blend. Add the warm tomatoes, the peeled fava beans, and the mint to the vinaigrette and toss to coat. Season with salt and pepper.

Preheat a heavy skillet or griddle to medium-high heat. Sprinkle the scallops with salt and pepper, and then rub the remaining 1 tablespoon olive oil over them. Arrange the scallops, seasoned side down, in the pan and cook for about 2 minutes without moving them. Sprinkle more salt and pepper over the scallops. Using a metal spatula, turn the scallops over and cook for another 2 minutes, or until they are just opaque in the center and golden-brown on both sides. The scallops shouldn't be cooked all the way through.

Spoon the salad onto the center of 4 plates, dividing it evenly. Place 3 scallops on top of each salad. Drizzle with the vinaigrette remaining in the bowl, and serve.

chapter four
something to eat on the sofa

Who hasn't felt overwhelmed by life at one time or another? On those days there's no better feeling than closing the front door, drawing the blinds, kicking off your shoes, and knowing you've got the rest of the day to do absolutely nothing. I always feel so relaxed and chilled out when I'm sprawled across my sofa, creating my own personal comfort zone with some delicious food and a pleasant diversion in the form of a game on TV or just a good book. Whether you've got the house to yourself and are tucked in with a soft blanket, listening to your favorite CD, or you're cuddled up next to your significant other watching a scary movie, I hereby declare that the sofa can be one of the nicest places to enjoy scrummy comfort food.

lozza's corn and
bacon muffins

There's something about walking into someone's home and smelling a treat baking in the oven. My mum always makes these special muffins for me whenever I am home. She is a great baker and taught me everything I know. These need to be eaten as soon as they come out of the oven; split them open and spread them with butter so it melts into the hot muffins.

Makes 12

12 ounces hardwood-smoked bacon, coarsely chopped

1 ear yellow corn, husked

2½ cups all-purpose flour

4 teaspoons baking powder

½ teaspoon salt

¼ teaspoon cayenne pepper

1¼ cups whole milk

3 large eggs

2 cups grated sharp white cheddar cheese

⅓ cup coarsely chopped fresh chives

Salted butter, for serving

Preheat the oven to 400°F. Cook the bacon in a large heavy sauté pan over medium heat for about 8 minutes, or until it is browned and crisp. Using a slotted spoon, transfer the bacon to paper towels. Brush 12 standard-size muffin cups generously with some of the bacon drippings from the pan, and set aside ½ cup of the remaining bacon drippings to cool slightly. Discard any remaining bacon fat.

Use a sharp knife to slice the corn kernels off the cob. You should have about 1 cup.

Whisk the flour, baking powder, salt, and cayenne pepper in a large bowl to blend. Whisk the milk, eggs, and reserved bacon drippings in another large bowl to blend; then stir in the bacon, 1½ cups of the cheese, the corn kernels, and the chives. Stir the milk mixture into the flour mixture just until blended. Spoon the batter into the prepared muffin cups, dividing it equally and mounding it generously. Sprinkle the tops of the muffins with the remaining ½ cup cheese. Bake for about 18 minutes, or until the muffins are golden and a tester inserted into the center of one comes out clean. Let the muffins cool slightly in the cups. Then run a small sharp knife around the muffins to loosen them from the cups, remove them, and serve them warm with salted butter.

baby baked potatoes with
sour cream and chives

Baked potatoes just might be the perfect comfort food. In miniature, they become a great finger food, too. Cooking the potatoes on a bed of salt dries them out a bit and gives them a fluffier, drier texture, so they can hold more of the good stuff like sour cream, butter, crispy bacon, grated cheese, or whatever tickles your fancy.

Serves 4

5 ounces coarse sea salt (about 1 cup)

2 sprigs fresh thyme

3 garlic cloves, crushed

12 small red-skinned potatoes, scrubbed

3 tablespoons olive oil

¼ cup sour cream

2 tablespoons chopped fresh chives

Preheat the oven to 375°F. Mix the salt, thyme, and garlic in a small bowl. Sprinkle the salt mixture into a roasting pan, arrange the potatoes on top of it, and drizzle the oil over the potatoes. Bake for about 25 minutes, or until the potatoes are fully cooked and soft. Remove the potatoes from the oven and let them cool.

Brush any excess salt mixture from the potatoes and cut a small X in the top of each one. Using both thumbs and index fingers, press inward to open the top of each potato. Dollop a teaspoon of sour cream onto each potato, sprinkle with the chives, and serve.

roasted eggplant dip
with crispy pita chips

Homemade dips always taste much better than the ones you buy, and this one is no exception. The eggplant is so creamy and the pita so crunchy—they were made for each other. If you're looking for a healthful snack, this is the one for you.

Serves 4

Eggplant dip

2 eggplants (about 2 pounds total)

4 teaspoons plus 2 tablespoons extra-virgin olive oil

1 head garlic, separated into cloves

3 tablespoons tahini

3 tablespoons chopped fresh flat-leaf parsley

2 tablespoons fresh lemon juice

Salt and freshly ground black pepper

Pita chips

3 pita breads, split horizontally in half

2 tablespoons olive oil

2 tablespoons chopped fresh flat-leaf parsley

Salt and freshly ground black pepper

For the eggplant dip: Preheat the oven to 400°F and preheat a grill pan over high heat. Prick the eggplants all over with a fork and rub them with 2 teaspoons of the olive oil. Place the eggplants on the hot grill pan and cook for 8 minutes, or until charred all over.

Meanwhile, place the garlic cloves on a sheet of foil and drizzle with 2 teaspoons of the olive oil. Fold in the edges of the foil to form a packet.

Place the grilled eggplants and the pouch of garlic on a baking sheet and bake for 45 minutes, or until the garlic is tender and golden and the eggplants are very tender. Remove the eggplants and garlic from the oven, and set aside to cool. Reduce the oven temperature to 375°F.

Remove and discard the skin from the eggplants and garlic. Cut the eggplants in half lengthwise and remove the seeds. Chop the eggplant pulp and garlic to form a coarse puree, and place in a large bowl. Stir in the tahini, parsley, lemon juice, and remaining 2 tablespoons olive oil. Season with salt and pepper to taste.

For the pita chips: Cut each pita half into wedges and arrange the wedges evenly over 2 large baking sheets. Brush the pita wedges with the olive oil, and sprinkle with the parsley and with salt and pepper to taste. Bake for 12 minutes, or until the pita wedges are crisp and golden. Let the chips cool, and serve with the eggplant dip.

Both the dip and the chips can be made ahead of time. Place them in airtight containers, and store the dip in the refrigerator for up to 3 days.

toasted walnut sourdough with melted gorgonzola and cranberry-fig preserve

The only thing better than Gorgonzola is Gorgonzola when it has melted and is oozing over some great sourdough bread and is topped with a sweet preserve. The walnuts bring a richness to this sandwich. See the photograph on page 105.

Serves 4 to 6

Cranberry-Fig Preserve

12 ounces fresh cranberries

8 ounces dried Black Mission figs, halved

½ cup sugar

1 cinnamon stick

Sandwiches

32 whole walnut halves

8 slices walnut-raisin sourdough bread, halved diagonally

8 ounces Gorgonzola cheese (Gorgonzola dolce)

To make the preserve: Combine the cranberries, figs, sugar, cinnamon stick, and 1 cup water in a medium-size heavy saucepan and simmer over medium-low heat, stirring occasionally, for about 25 minutes, or until the mixture thickens and the figs soften. Let the preserve cool completely, and remove cinnamon stick. (You can make the preserve up to 2 weeks ahead of time.)

Preheat the broiler. Place the walnuts in a single layer on a baking sheet and broil for 3 to 5 minutes, or until golden brown, tossing once or twice. Remove the walnuts and reserve them for the garnish. Arrange the bread slices on the baking sheet and broil until golden and crisp on top. Turn the bread slices over and spread the cheese on the untoasted side. Broil for 15 seconds, or until the cheese is just beginning to melt. Spoon some of the preserve onto each piece of toast, garnish with the walnuts, and serve.

sticky chicken drumsticks

The first time I made this, I served it to a group of kids and watched them become instantly mesmerized as they devoured their dinner. Okay, so I've learned to serve them with napkins. I guess I am still a big kid.

Serves 4 to 6

¼ cup soy sauce

¼ cup Chinese barbecue sauce (*char sui*)

¼ cup honey

3 garlic cloves, finely chopped

1 tablespoon finely chopped peeled fresh ginger

12 chicken drumsticks

2 teaspoons sesame seeds, toasted

Mix the soy sauce, barbecue sauce, honey, garlic, and ginger in a resealable storage bag to blend. Add the chicken, seal the bag, and toss to coat with the sauce. Refrigerate for at least 1 hour but preferably overnight.

Position an oven rack 8 to 10 inches from the heat source and preheat the broiler. Line a large, rimmed baking sheet with heavy-duty foil. Transfer the drumsticks and marinade to the prepared baking sheet and broil, turning the drumsticks occasionally and watching them closely, for 25 minutes, or until the chicken is cooked through and the marinade has glazed it. Sprinkle the sesame seeds over the chicken, and serve.

smoked trout melt
with cucumber on pumpernickel

The grilled cheese sandwiches from our childhoods always manage to put smiles on our faces, and even though the ingredients in this version are a bit more sophisticated, the effect is the same. You get a lot of flavors and textures in every bite of this open-face sandwich: hot and cool, and tangy and smoky. Once the smoked trout and the cheese melt together, it goes all gooey and delicious. Yum, yum, yum.

Serves 4

10 ounces smoked trout, skin and any bones removed

$1/2$ cup crème fraîche

1 cornichon, finely diced

$1 1/2$ tablespoons chopped fresh dill

$1 1/2$ tablespoons fresh lemon juice

Salt and freshly ground black pepper

4 slices pumpernickel (or rye) bread

$1/4$ cucumber, thinly sliced

4 slices Emmentaler cheese

Preheat the broiler. Flake the trout into large chunks and toss them in a medium bowl with the crème fraîche, cornichon, 1 tablespoon of the dill, and the lemon juice. Season with salt and pepper to taste.

Arrange the pumpernickel bread slices in a single layer on a baking sheet and broil for about 1 minute on each side. Arrange the cucumber slices on the pieces of toast, and spoon the trout mixture over the cucumbers. Return the sandwiches to the broiler for about 2 minutes, or until the trout mixture is warm. Top the sandwiches with the cheese and broil again for about 3 minutes, or until the cheese has melted and is lightly golden. Sprinkle with the remaining $1/2$ tablespoon dill, and serve.

roasted beef fillet crostini
with arugula pesto

These aren't dainty little nibbles; they are more like an open-face sandwich. Arugula pesto is a little spicier than a regular basil pesto, especially with a kick of fresh horseradish, and its flavor works really well with rare roasted beef. Make up a big plate of these and set them on the table for a no-pressure snack.

Makes 24 crostini

Arugula pesto

1½ cups (lightly packed) fresh arugula leaves

⅓ cup pine nuts, toasted (see Note, page 223)

1 tablespoon freshly grated fresh horseradish (see Note)

½ cup freshly grated Parmesan cheese

½ cup extra-virgin olive oil

Salt and freshly ground black pepper

Crostini

1 loaf ciabatta bread

4 tablespoons olive oil

Salt and freshly ground black pepper

One 2-pound beef tenderloin, silver skin or sinew removed

4 sprigs fresh rosemary

1 cup fresh arugula

To prepare the pesto: Combine the arugula, pine nuts, and horseradish in a food processor and pulse until the nuts are finely chopped. Add the Parmesan cheese, and slowly blend in the extra-virgin olive oil. Season with salt and pepper to taste. Set the pesto aside.

To prepare the crostini: Preheat the oven to 400°F. Thinly slice the ciabatta crosswise into twenty-four ¼-inch-thick slices, and arrange the slices in a single layer on 2 large baking sheets. Drizzle with 2 tablespoons of the olive oil and season with salt and pepper. Toast in the oven for 5 minutes, or until they are slightly golden. Remove from the oven and let cool. Maintain the oven temperature.

Cut the fillet lengthwise into 4 even pieces. Place a large ovenproof frying pan over high heat until very hot. While it heats, sprinkle the pieces of beef evenly on all sides with salt and pepper, and drizzle with the remaining 2 tablespoons olive oil. Place the beef and the rosemary sprigs in the hot pan and cook until the beef is brown on all sides but still rare in the center, about 6 minutes total. Then place the pan with the beef in the oven for 2 minutes. Remove the pan from the oven and let the beef rest in the pan for 5 minutes. Discard the rosemary.

Using a sharp knife, thinly slice the beef fillets crosswise. Arrange the arugula leaves atop the crostini. Top with the beef slices, and then drizzle the pesto over the beef.

Note
Fresh horseradish is available in many produce sections, and somewhat resembles a parsnip. Its pungent flavor is miles better than the bottled kind, so do seek it out.

honey-glazed ham panini

Make this as one big Scooby Doo–style panino and then chop it up or tear it up as you like. The pear and mustard chutney is great to make in double batches so you can keep some in the fridge—as it's the perfect accompaniment to roasted meats.

Serves 6

Pear and mustard chutney

1 cup apple cider vinegar

¾ cup (packed) light brown sugar

1 small onion, finely chopped

¼ cup coarse-grain mustard

Grated zest of 1 orange

4 Anjou pears, peeled, cored, and coarsely chopped

Sliders

1 large loaf focaccia (about 17 x 6 x 1½ inches)

1 pound honey-glazed ham, cut into slices

8 ounces sliced Swiss cheese

3 ounces fresh baby spinach leaves (about 3 cups)

1 tablespoon butter, at room temperature

To make the chutney: Combine the vinegar, brown sugar, onions, mustard, and orange zest in a heavy saucepan, and bring to a boil over medium heat. Then reduce the heat and simmer for about 20 minutes, or until the onions are tender and the liquid has thickened slightly. Add the pears and continue simmering gently for about 30 minutes, or until the pears soften and the liquid thickens some more. Let the chutney cool, and then keep it in the refrigerator in an airtight container. (The chutney will keep for up to a week.)

To make the sliders: Position an oven rack 8 inches from the heat source and preheat the broiler. Cut the bread in half horizontally and arrange the halves, cut side up, on 2 baking sheets. Place the ham and cheese over one of the bread halves. Toast both bread halves under the broiler for 2 minutes, or until the cheese melts and the uncovered bread is golden brown.

Scatter the spinach over the ham and cheese. Spoon the chutney over the spinach. Top with the second bread half. Brush the top of the slider with the butter and broil for 1 minute, or until the top is crisp. Cut the slider into 12 pieces, and serve.

barbecue chicken
quesadillas

I know this isn't the kind of recipe that you'd expect from a chef who has worked in Michelin-starred restaurants, but this quesadilla is one of my guilty pleasures. If you've got some tortillas and a bit of leftover roasted chicken in the fridge, you have the makings of the ultimate sofa snack. If you've come across a fantastic store-bought barbecue sauce, feel free to use that instead.

Serves 4

Four 10-inch-diameter flour tortillas

2 cups (about 8 ounces) coarsely shredded roasted chicken

2 cups (about 6 ounces) grated Monterey Jack cheese

½ cup coarsely chopped fresh cilantro

1 jalapeño, finely chopped

Salt

¼ cup barbecue sauce (see All-American Barbecued Baby Back Ribs, page 192 and Slowly Cooked Brisket with a BBQ Bourbon Sauce, page 196)

Preheat the oven to 250°F.

Arrange the tortillas on a work surface. Divide the chicken, cheese, cilantro, and jalapeño among the tortillas, scattering the ingredients over half of each tortilla. Sprinkle with salt and drizzle a tablespoon of barbecue sauce over each. Fold the uncovered half of each tortilla over the filling to form a half-moon shape.

Heat a large flat griddle pan over medium heat. Place 2 quesadillas on the griddle. Cook for about 3 minutes on each side, or until the tortillas are crisp and golden and the cheese has melted. Transfer the quesadillas to a baking sheet and keep them warm in the oven. Repeat with the remaining 2 quesadillas. Cut the quesadillas into wedges, and serve.

fresh crab and avocado dip
with crispy tortilla chips

Crab and avocado is an age-old combination that has a bit of magic to it, which is why you see it in so many cuisines, from Asian to Italian. I'd never thought to make tortilla chips until I came to America, but they are *so* much better than store-bought. Salt them the minute they come out of the hot oil.

Serves 6

4 firm but ripe avocados, peeled, pitted, and coarsely chopped

¼ cup sour cream

4 tablespoons fresh lime juice

2 tablespoons finely chopped fresh chives

Salt and freshly ground black pepper

1 cup fresh crabmeat

½ cup mayonnaise

3 tablespoons thinly sliced fresh basil

1 red jalapeño, finely chopped

Canola oil, for deep-frying

12 fresh corn tortillas, cut into 8 wedges each

Fresh basil leaves, for garnish

Mash the avocados, sour cream, 3 tablespoons of the lime juice, and the chives in a large bowl. Season the avocado mixture with salt and pepper to taste. Spoon the mixture into a clear glass serving bowl, forming an even layer and smoothing the top.

Squeeze the crabmeat gently to remove any excess liquid, and pick through it to remove any bits of shell or cartilage. Gently mix the crabmeat, mayonnaise, sliced basil, jalapeño, and the remaining 1 tablespoon lime juice in another bowl. Season with salt and pepper to taste. Spoon the crab mixture over the avocado mixture, forming a second even layer and smoothing the top. Cover and refrigerate until ready to serve.

Heat 3 inches of oil in a wok or deep skillet over medium-high heat. Working in batches, add the tortilla wedges and fry, stirring often so that they cook evenly on both sides, for about 3 minutes, or until they are crisp and golden brown. Using a slotted spoon or a mesh strainer, transfer the corn chips to paper towels to drain any excess oil. While the chips are still hot, sprinkle them lightly with salt.

Garnish the dip with basil leaves, and serve with the tortilla chips.

homemade salted caramel popcorn

I make this when I've asked some mates around to watch a movie or a game. The whole house smells great the minute they walk in the door, and it's so delicious that they don't stop eating it until it's gone. There is nothing like the smell and taste of freshly popped popcorn. I'd tell you that this will last until the following day, but I'd be lying; you'll be lucky if it lasts an hour!

Makes about 24 cups

2 tablespoons canola oil
¾ cup popcorn kernels
2 cups sugar
1¼ teaspoons sea salt

Spray 2 large, rimmed baking sheets with nonstick cooking spray. Heat the oil in a large heavy pot over medium-high heat until it is hot but not smoking. Add the popcorn kernels and cover the pot. Using pot holders, shake the pot constantly over the heat as the kernels pop, about 5 minutes, or until the kernels stop popping. Immediately spread the popcorn out on the prepared baking sheets.

Stir the sugar, salt, and ¼ cup water in a small heavy saucepan over low heat until the sugar dissolves, occasionally brushing down the sides of the pan with a wet pastry brush. Increase the heat and boil without stirring, occasionally brushing down the sides and swirling the pan, until the syrup is a deep amber color, about 8 minutes.

Working quickly, drizzle the hot caramel over the popcorn and toss with 2 wooden spoons to coat the popcorn lightly. Be careful not to get hot caramel on your skin. Allow the caramel corn to cool slightly, and run for the sofa.

chapter five
daily dinners

Even professional chefs face the question of what to cook after a busy day at work, and no one wants to spend precious time running across town to specialty stores for exotic ingredients on a weeknight. Fortunately, it's actually quite easy to pull together a tasty dinner in around thirty minutes with ingredients that you can find readily at your local grocery store.

Weeknight cooking really doesn't have to be hard work. The lure of frozen dinners and take-out food may seem appealing, but in the time that it would take you to order and pick up your pre-prepared food, you could have cooked any one of the recipes from this chapter—*really!* When I am invited to someone's home for a meal, I love the feeling of walking through the door and getting a whiff of whatever they've been preparing; it piques my appetite and instills a healthy appreciation for the person who has cooked dinner. All that gets lost if you simply opt for takeout.

And really, why would you go that route when you can put any of these delicious dinners in your weekly repertoire? None of them will keep you chained to the kitchen, and all will provide the perfect transition between a hectic day and the relaxed evening ahead.

asparagus and parmesan risotto

Risotto is the ultimate one-pot wonder, and it's the perfect dish to cook with a glass of wine in your hand—have a sip, have a stir, have a sip, have a stir. Stirring every thirty seconds or so and adding the stock gradually ensures that your risotto will be creamy, not porridge-y. Risotto can tend to be a little heavy, but asparagus and mint lighten it up, making it a great dish for spring.

Serves 4

About 8 cups store-bought vegetable stock

2 tablespoons olive oil

3 shallots, finely diced

2 garlic cloves, finely chopped

3 sprigs fresh thyme

2 cups Arborio rice

¾ cup dry white wine

1½ pounds thin asparagus, woody ends removed, stalks cut into 1½-inch lengths

4 tablespoons (½ stick) butter, cut in small pieces

½ cup grated Parmigiano-Reggiano cheese

¼ cup mascarpone cheese

2 tablespoons finely chopped fresh flat-leaf parsley

¼ cup finely chopped fresh mint leaves

Juice of ½ lemon

Sea salt and freshly ground black pepper

Parmigiano-Reggiano cheese, shaved with a vegetable peeler, for garnish

Bring the vegetable stock to a simmer in a large saucepan. Reduce the heat to very low and keep the stock on the heat.

Heat the oil in a large heavy saucepan over medium heat. Add the shallots, garlic, and thyme, and sauté for 2 minutes, or until the shallots are tender but not browned. Add the rice and sauté for 30 seconds to coat with the oil. Stir in the wine and cook for 3 minutes, or until it is absorbed. Add ¾ cup of the hot vegetable stock and cook, stirring constantly, until it has been absorbed. Continue adding the hot stock, ¾ cup at a time, stirring until each addition has been absorbed, for about 22 minutes, or until the rice is al dente (the center of each grain of rice should still be slightly firm).

Add the asparagus and continue to cook for 2 minutes. Discard the thyme stems (the thyme leaves should have fallen off the stems and into the risotto). Remove the risotto from the heat, and add the butter, grated Parmigiano-Reggiano, and mascarpone cheese. Stir until the butter has melted. Then stir in the parsley, mint, and lemon juice, and season the risotto generously with salt and pepper.

Divide the risotto among 4 warmed serving bowls. Garnish with the shaved Parmigiano-Reggiano, and serve.

fresh linguine with garlic shrimp
and homemade pesto

This satisfying dish just takes minutes to put together. Despite the speedy preparation, it seems really indulgent and tastes fresh and healthy at the same time. When making pesto, you can vary the consistency to match the purpose: Make it nice and thick to spread over bruschetta, or thin it with extra olive oil so it's easy to toss through pasta, as in this version.

Serves 4

Pesto

1½ cups (lightly packed) fresh basil leaves

½ cup pine nuts, toasted (see Note on page 223)

½ cup freshly grated Parmesan cheese

¼ cup extra-virgin olive oil

Salt and freshly ground black pepper

Linguine

12 cherry tomatoes on the vine

4 tablespoons extra-virgin olive oil

Salt and freshly ground black pepper

9 ounces fresh linguine (from the dairy case)

2 garlic cloves, minced

20 large shrimp, peeled and deveined

Parmesan shavings, for garnish

To make the pesto: Grind the basil, pine nuts, and grated Parmesan cheese with a mortar and pestle until a smooth paste forms. (If you don't have a mortar and pestle, use a food processor instead.) Slowly add the olive oil, grinding until a smooth sauce forms. Season the pesto with salt and pepper to taste. Then cover and set it aside.

Preheat the oven to 450°F. Place the vine of tomatoes in an ovenproof skillet. Drizzle 1 tablespoon of the oil over the tomatoes, and sprinkle them with salt and pepper. Roast the tomatoes in the oven for 8 minutes, or until heated through.

Meanwhile, bring a large pot of salted water to a boil over high heat. Add the linguine and cook, stirring occasionally to prevent it from sticking, for about 2 minutes, or until al dente.

While the linguine cooks, heat the remaining 3 tablespoons olive oil in a medium sauté pan over medium heat. Add the garlic and shrimp and sauté for about 3 minutes, or until the shrimp are just cooked through and the garlic is tender. Stir the pesto into the shrimp mixture.

Drain the linguine, reserving about ½ cup of the cooking liquid. Toss the linguine in a large bowl with the shrimp-pesto mixture, adding enough of the reserved cooking liquid to moisten the sauce so that it coats the pasta evenly.

Using a two-pronged carving fork, swirl some pasta around the fork. Slide it off the fork, letting it mound in the center of a plate. Repeat. Arrange the shrimp and the roasted tomatoes around the pasta. Garnish with the cheese and serve.

rigatoni with spicy italian salami, baby tomatoes, olives, and capers

For all its simplicity, this is an intensely flavored pasta dish that packs a real punch. Serve it for lunch or dinner with a very simple salad; you don't want a lot of complicated flavors to compete with the sauce.

Serves 4

20 cherry tomatoes on the vine

2 teaspoons plus 1 tablespoon extra-virgin olive oil

Salt and freshly ground black pepper

8 ounces spicy salami, such as Sopressa Vicentina, sliced

2 garlic cloves, minced

¼ cup dry white wine

¼ cup pitted kalamata olives

¼ cup extra-fine capers

¼ cup coarsely chopped fresh flat-leaf parsley

8 to 10 ounces rigatoni pasta

Preheat the oven to 375°F. Place the tomatoes on a small baking sheet and drizzle with the 2 teaspoons olive oil. Sprinkle with salt and pepper. Roast the tomatoes in the oven for about 8 minutes, or until they begin to split. Remove the tomatoes from the oven and let them cool slightly.

Bring a large pot of salted water to a boil.

While the water is heating, heat the remaining 1 tablespoon oil in a large heavy sauté pan over medium heat. Add the salami and cook for 30 seconds on each side, until light golden in color. Remove the salami from the pan and reserve.

Return the pan to the heat, add the garlic, and sauté for 1 minute, or until tender. Add the tomatoes and sauté for 3 minutes. Add the wine and simmer for about 3 minutes, or until reduced by about half. Add the olives and capers and toss gently. Bring the mixture to a simmer and add the salami and parsley.

Meanwhile, cook the pasta in the boiling salted water for 8 minutes, or until al dente. Drain the pasta and toss it in the pan with the sauce. Season the pasta to taste with salt and pepper. Transfer the pasta to plates, spooning any extra salami and tomato mixture from the pan around the pasta, and serve.

mussels and snapper steamed in coconut milk

All the delicious flavors of Southeast Asia are at work here: lemongrass, cilantro, and ginger along with coconut milk. They add up to a dish that is creamy and fresh at the same time, and decadent without being heavy. When the mussels open up, they add their rich flavor to the broth—it's really a fabulous dish!

Serves 4

One 2-inch piece fresh lemongrass

2 tablespoons olive oil

24 mussels, scrubbed and debearded (see Note)

2 red jalapeños, finely chopped

One 1-inch piece fresh ginger, peeled and finely chopped

2 garlic cloves, finely chopped

4 baby bok choy, halved lengthwise, leaves separated

¼ cup sweet white wine (such as Gewürztraminer)

½ cup coconut water (see Note, page 19)

Four 6-ounce red snapper fillets

½ cup canned unsweetened coconut milk

Salt and freshly ground black pepper

½ bunch fresh cilantro, for garnish

Using the dull side of a large sharp knife, pound the lemongrass to break it apart and help release its aroma. Place a large wok or skillet over medium heat and add the oil. Add the lemongrass, mussels, jalapeños, ginger, and garlic and toss to mix. Cover the wok for 2 to 3 minutes to allow the steam to build up and cook the mussels. Then add the bok choy, wine, and coconut water and toss to combine. Place the snapper fillets on a wire rack and set the rack over the mussels. Cover and steam for about 5 minutes, or until the fish is just cooked through and the mussels have opened. Discard any mussels that do not open. Add the coconut milk to the mussels and toss well. Season the sauce with salt and pepper to taste.

Arrange the mussels around the outsides of 4 wide bowls. Place the bok choy and snapper in the middle of the bowls. Pour the sauce over the fish and mussels. Garnish with the cilantro, and serve.

Note
To debeard the mussels, first use the back of a spoon to clean off any barnacles. You may see a small tuft of what looks like a little beard—hence the name. Pull the beard off the mussel and discard it. If you can't find a beard, it simply means the mussels have already been prepared for you by the fishmonger.

steamed mussels with chorizo and white wine

Mussels and chorizo is a classic Spanish combination that is hard to improve on. This is the kind of dish to savor around the table for a good long while, dunking pieces of bread into all those delicious juices in the bottom of the bowl. You should buy the mussels the same day you are going to cook them: The fresher they are, the better they will taste. Mussels cook in less than twenty minutes, so you can have dinner on the table in next to no time.

Serves 4

1 pound Spanish chorizo, cut into bite-size pieces

4 shallots, finely chopped

2 garlic cloves, finely chopped

4 pounds mussels, scrubbed and debearded (see Note, page 139)

1 cup dry white wine

3 tablespoons finely chopped fresh cilantro, plus more for garnish

6 tablespoons (¾ stick) butter, cut into pieces

1 baguette, torn into large pieces

Place a large wide pot over medium heat. Add the chorizo and sauté for about 8 minutes, or until it is golden brown. Add the shallots and garlic, and sauté for about 2 minutes, or until fragrant. Add the mussels and toss quickly to coat. Add the wine. Cover the pot and cook over medium-high heat for about 3 minutes, or until the mussels begin to open. Discard any mussels that do not open. Add the 3 table-spoons cilantro, and toss to combine.

Using a slotted spoon, transfer the mussels and sausages to a warmed large serving bowl. Cover to keep warm. Boil the juices remaining in the pan for 1 minute. Then whisk in the butter. Pour the sauce over the mussels, sprinkle with the additional cilantro, and serve immediately with the baguette pieces.

oven-roasted monkfish
with garlic mashed potatoes and pinot noir reduction

When I lived in Europe, monkfish was an expensive and prized fish, so I was thrilled to discover that in the States it's still quite reasonable, allowing me to eat it whenever I want—which is often. Monkfish has a really meaty texture, so it can easily stand up to the kind of accompaniments you would normally serve with a steak, like a red wine reduction and hearty mashed potatoes.

Serves 4

One 750-ml bottle Pinot Noir

2 large russet potatoes
(about 2 pounds total), peeled

6 large garlic cloves, unpeeled

2/3 cup whole milk

1/4 cup heavy cream

10 tablespoons butter

Sea salt and freshly ground
black pepper

1 tablespoon olive oil

Four 6- to 7-ounce monkfish
fillets (preferably the thick
end of the fillets)

Juice of 1/2 lemon

Pour the wine into a medium-size heavy saucepan and bring to a boil. Simmer over medium-high heat for 40 minutes, or until reduced to 1/3 cup and slightly thick.

Meanwhile, cut the potatoes into 2-inch chunks, and place them in a large saucepan of salted water. Bring to a boil and cook for about 15 minutes, or until tender.

While the potatoes are cooking, cook the garlic in a small saucepan of boiling water for 1 minute; then remove and dunk in a bowl of cold water. Repeat this blanching process two more times. Peel off the garlic skins and mash the garlic into a puree, using the bottom of a saucer or a mortar and pestle.

Drain the potatoes well. Then return them to the pan and mash, or press them through a potato ricer into a second pan. Mix the mashed garlic into the mashed potatoes.

Bring the milk to a simmer in a small saucepan over medium-high heat; then slowly stir it into the mashed potatoes. Slowly stir in the cream to make a nice, velvety-smooth puree. Cook over medium-low heat for 5 minutes, and

gradually beat in 5 tablespoons of the butter. Season the potatoes with salt and pepper to taste. Cover the potatoes with cling film so a skin doesn't form. Keep warm.

Heat the oil in a large heavy frying pan over medium-high heat. Sprinkle the monkfish with salt and pepper. Place the monkfish in the frying pan and cook without turning for about 8 minutes, or until it is just firm to the touch and almost cooked through. Turn the fish over, and add the lemon juice and remaining 5 tablespoons butter to the pan. Continue cooking the monkfish on the second side, spooning the lemon-butter over the fish as it cooks, for about 4 minutes, or until the fish is just cooked through.

Place some of the potato puree in the centers of 4 plates and set the monkfish on top of the potatoes. Drizzle the wine reduction around the potatoes and over the fish, and serve.

grilled tuna with fennel, onions, parsley, and lemon

The most important piece of advice to remember about this dish is to get the pan bloody hot before you add the fish—you really can't get it too hot! That way the tuna will get nicely colored on the outside while remaining beautifully rare and just barely warm on the inside. If you haven't come across caper berries yet, give them a try. Their flavor is similar to capers but with a bit of crunch from the seeds. If you can't find both the berries and the capers, just use one or the other.

Serves 4

Caramelized fennel and onions

4 fennel bulbs, each trimmed and cut into 6 wedges

1 tablespoon olive oil

1 onion, sliced crosswise into ¼-inch-thick rings

½ cup pitted kalamata olives

½ cup drained caper berries

2 tablespoons drained extra-fine capers

2 tablespoons chopped fresh flat-leaf parsley

Juice of 2 lemons

1 garlic clove, chopped

5 tablespoons extra-virgin olive oil

Salt and freshly ground black pepper

Fish

Four 6-ounce ahi (yellowfin) tuna fillets

1 tablespoon olive oil

Salt and freshly ground black pepper

To prepare the caramelized fennel and onions: Preheat the oven to 400°F. Toss the fennel wedges with the olive oil. Preheat a grill pan over medium-high heat, add the fennel and onions, and grill until grill marks appear. Place in a 13 x 9-inch baking dish. Add the olives, caper berries, fine capers, parsley, lemon juice, and garlic, and toss well to combine. Roast for 15 to 20 minutes, or until the vegetables are tender and the flavors have blended. Remove from the oven and drizzle with the extra-virgin olive oil. Season with salt and pepper, and keep warm.

To cook the fish: Heat a large grill pan over high heat until very hot. Coat the fish fillets with the oil, and sprinkle with salt and pepper to taste. Cook the fish for 2 to 3 minutes on each side, or until it is seared on the outside but still rare in the center. (The cooking time may vary, depending on the size and thickness of the fillets.)

Spoon the fennel mixture onto the centers of 4 plates. Place the fish on top of the fennel mixture. Drizzle any juices from the vegetables around the fish and onto the plates, and serve.

crispy-skin salmon salad with roasted cherry tomatoes

Salmon is a great source of thiamin, protein, and omega-3 fatty acids. I have to say, I love roasted cherry tomatoes and use them in virtually everything I cook; their sweet yet slightly acidic flavor is perfect with the salmon.

Serves 4

16 cherry tomatoes on the vine

2 teaspoons plus ¼ cup extra-virgin olive oil

Salt and freshly ground black pepper

Four 6-ounce salmon fillets, skin on

½ cup fresh lime juice

¼ cup grapeseed oil

4 ounces mixed baby lettuce leaves

Preheat the oven to 375°F. Place the tomatoes on a small baking sheet and drizzle with the 2 teaspoons olive oil. Sprinkle with salt and pepper. Roast the tomatoes in the oven for about 8 minutes, or until they begin to split. Remove the tomatoes from the oven and let them cool slightly.

Meanwhile, using a sharp knife, score the salmon fillets. Sprinkle the salmon with salt and pepper. Place the salmon, skin side down, in a cold, large heavy nonstick sauté pan. Place the pan over medium-low heat. Increase the heat to high and cook the salmon for 2 to 3 minutes, or until the skin is golden brown. Turn the salmon over and cook for 1 to 2 minutes longer, or until the salmon is just pink in the middle.

Place the lime juice in a bowl and slowly whisk in the grapeseed oil and the remaining ¼ cup olive oil. Season with salt and pepper. Mound the lettuce leaves into chef's rings (see Note) on 4 plates, or stack the lettuce in the centers of the plates. Arrange the crispy-skin salmon and roasted tomatoes over the salads. Drizzle some of the vinaigrette over the salmon and salads, and serve.

Note

Chef's rings are short, hollow tubes similar to a 3-inch-round cookie or biscuit cutter. They are available at kitchenware stores.

pan-fried halibut with black beans
and cilantro-chile salsa

Take a beautiful piece of fish, add some black beans, and you have a dish that's full of protein and very healthy to boot.

Serves 4

Salsa

¼ cup extra-virgin olive oil

2 tablespoons red wine vinegar

⅓ cup chopped fresh cilantro

3 serrano chiles, seeded and finely chopped

1 shallot, finely diced

2 garlic cloves, finely chopped

Salt

Black beans and halibut:

4 tablespoons extra-virgin olive oil

1 small red onion, diced

½ red bell pepper, seeded and diced

½ green bell pepper, seeded and diced

½ yellow bell pepper, seeded and diced

1 garlic clove, finely crushed

One 15-ounce can black beans, drained and rinsed

½ cup dry white wine

2 tablespoons chopped fresh flat-leaf parsley

Salt and freshly ground black pepper

Four 6-ounce halibut fillets

To make the salsa: Stir the oil, vinegar, cilantro, chiles, shallots, and garlic in a medium bowl to combine. Season the salsa to taste with salt, and set it aside at room temperature to let the flavors develop.

To make the beans: Heat 2 tablespoons of the oil in a large sauté pan over medium heat. Add the red onions and sauté for 5 minutes, or until tender. Add all the bell peppers and the garlic, and sauté for 5 minutes, or until the bell peppers soften. Add the beans and the wine. Bring the wine to a gentle simmer and cook for about 3 minutes, or until the beans are heated through and most of the wine has reduced. Stir in the parsley, and season with salt and pepper. Keep warm.

To make the halibut: Place a large sauté or frying pan over medium-high heat and drizzle the remaining 2 tablespoons oil into it. Sprinkle both sides of the halibut fillets with salt and pepper. Place the fillets in the hot pan and cook for 4 minutes, or until they are golden brown on the bottom. Turn the fillets over and cook for 3 minutes, or until the fish is just cooked through but still moist and juicy.

Spoon the beans onto the centers of 4 plates. Top with the halibut fillets. Spoon some salsa atop the halibut, drizzle a bit more salsa around the beans, and serve.

braised daurade with roasted tomatoes, bell peppers, olives, and capers

Daurade is the French name for sea bream, a flaky white-fleshed fish that is very succulent and tasty. It cooks and tastes like snapper or branzino, either of which you could substitute here. If you've never cooked a whole fish before, this is a great one to try. You just make a simple tomato sauce in a pan, place the whole fish on top, and thirty minutes later it's ready to eat! To save time, you can make the tomato sauce a few days ahead (it's a great thing to have on hand, anyway, for quick pasta meals), or even use a good-quality store-bought sauce.

When you get the fish, ask your fishmonger (nicely, of course!) to make doubly sure there are no scales left on it—a stray scale can really ruin the meal.

Serves 4

4 tablespoons olive oil

1 onion, coarsely diced

1 garlic clove, crushed

1 red bell pepper, seeded and coarsely diced

3 sprigs fresh basil, leaves only, coarsely chopped

1 sprig fresh oregano, leaves only, finely chopped

1 red jalapeño, finely chopped

1¼ cups dry white wine

6 vine-ripened tomatoes (about 2 pounds total), coarsely diced

Heat 3 tablespoons of the oil in a large heavy frying pan over medium heat. Add the onions and garlic, and sauté for about 8 minutes, or until soft. Add the bell peppers, basil, oregano, and jalapeño, and sauté for 5 minutes, or until the peppers are tender. Add the wine to the pan, scraping the brown bits from the bottom, and simmer for 10 minutes, or until the liquid has reduced by half. Add the tomatoes and simmer gently for about 35 minutes. (You may need to top the sauce up with a little water as it is cooking—you will know to do this if the sauce is getting so thick that it begins to stick to the bottom and turn a little brown.) Remove the sauce from the heat and add the olives and capers.

Using a large sharp knife, cut three slashes into each side of the whole fish. Place the 2 whole fish on the tomato sauce and cover the pan with a tight-fitting lid. Return the pan to medium heat and cook for 30 minutes, or until the fish flesh comes away from the bone easily.

¼ cup pitted kalamata olives

¼ cup drained extra-fine capers

2 large whole daurades (about 1½ pounds each), cleaned and scaled

12 ounces fresh baby spinach leaves

Salt and freshly ground black pepper

Meanwhile, heat the remaining 1 tablespoon oil in a large heavy sauté pan over medium-high heat. Add the spinach and season with salt and pepper. Sauté the spinach for 2 minutes, or just until it wilts.

Spoon the spinach onto a platter, and arrange the fish alongside. Spoon the tomato sauce over and around the fish, and serve.

When you are at the table, the best way to get the fish off the bone is to use a knife and fork and gently cut the fillets away from the bone, starting at the head end of the fish and working from the back to the belly. Don't be scared to make a mess—it's part of the fun.

red curry with lobster and pineapple

This curry is doubly rich from the coconut milk and the deep red curry, but the pineapple keeps it from being too heavy and gives a beautiful freshness to the dish. I like to cook the lobster in the shell because it makes for a more flavorful sauce, and I like to serve it that way too. You can be as refined as you like or, like me, pick up the shell and make an animal of yourself. If lobster is going to blow the budget, you can still have a delicious curry by substituting shrimp or monkfish.

Serves 4

One 14-ounce can unsweetened coconut milk

2 tablespoons red curry paste

1½ tablespoons fish sauce (*nam pla*)

1 (packed) tablespoon grated palm sugar (jaggery) or light brown sugar

8 ounces Chinese long beans or green beans, ends trimmed

4 slices peeled fresh ginger

2 kaffir lime leaves or the grated zest of 1 lime

1½ teaspoons tamarind paste

1½ cups bite-size cubes peeled fresh pineapple (about ¼ pineapple)

Two 8-ounce uncooked deveined lobster tails in the shell, split lengthwise

½ cup fresh basil leaves

Salt

Hot steamed rice, for serving

Simmer ¼ cup of the coconut milk in a large heavy saucepan over medium heat for 5 minutes, or until the oil separates from the milk. Stir in the curry paste and cook for 1 minute. Add the fish sauce and sugar, and cook, stirring constantly, for 2 minutes, or until the mixture darkens and thickens. Add the green beans and stir to coat. Add the remaining coconut milk and stir to scrape up the browned bits on the bottom of the pan. Stir in the ginger, lime leaves, and tamarind paste. Add the pineapple and simmer, stirring occasionally, for 3 minutes, or until the sauce reduces and thickens slightly and the beans are crisp-tender. Add the lobster and basil leaves and cook for 4 minutes, or until the lobster is just cooked through.

Discard the ginger and the lime leaves. Season the curry with salt to taste. Transfer one half lobster tail to each warmed serving bowl, and spoon the curry over it. Serve the steamed rice on the side.

crumbed chicken breasts
filled with swiss cheese

When I was cooking at a Michelin-starred restaurant, I served this dish—with a bit of prosciutto and shaved truffle added to the filling—and people went wild for it. It's really not much more involved than a simple pan-sautéed chicken, but it is much more impressive on the plate. I like the way the chicken breast looks with the wing bone still attached, but that's just me being a chef—it tastes equally good with or without the bone.

Serves 4

Four 8-ounce organic boneless, skinless chicken breasts, preferably with the wing attached and the wing bone trimmed (you can ask your butcher to do this)

One 4-ounce piece of Swiss cheese, such as Emmentaler, cut into four 3-inch sticks

Salt and freshly ground black pepper

½ cup all-purpose flour

2 large eggs

¾ cup plain dry breadcrumbs

5 tablespoons olive oil

2 cups broccoli florets

Preheat the oven to 350°F. Place the chicken breasts on a work surface with the smooth side of the breasts facing down. Gently fold back the tenderloin fillet while keeping it attached along the outer edge. (The tenderloin is the long strip of meat that runs down the length of the breast and tapers at the end.) Using the tip of a sharp knife, cut a small pocket into the thick portion of each chicken breast, from the center toward the thick end of the breast, away from the tenderloin, making a pocket that is large enough to fit a piece of cheese. Insert the cheese into the pockets. Fold the tenderloin fillet back over the pocket. Sprinkle the chicken breasts with salt and pepper.

Place the flour in a shallow bowl. Whisk the eggs to blend in another shallow bowl. Place the breadcrumbs in a third shallow bowl. Working with 1 chicken breast at a time, lightly dust the chicken breasts with the flour. Then carefully dip them into the egg to coat. Finally, coat the chicken breasts with the breadcrumbs. (See Note, page 157.)

Place a very large ovenproof nonstick sauté pan over medium heat. (If the pan is not large enough to fit all of the chicken breasts at one time, use 2 sauté pans.) Drizzle

3 tablespoons of the olive oil into the hot pan. Place the chicken breasts, tenderloin side up, in the hot pan and fry slowly for about 5 minutes, or until the breadcrumbs are golden brown on the bottom. Turn the chicken breasts over. Drizzle the remaining 2 tablespoons olive oil around the chicken breasts, and gently shake the pan to ensure that the oil coats the bottom of the pan.

Transfer the pan to the oven and bake the chicken breasts for about 10 minutes, or until they are cooked through and the cheese has melted. Using pot holders, remove the pan from the oven and let the chicken breasts rest for about 4 minutes.

Meanwhile, bring a large pot of water to a rapid boil. Add the broccoli florets and cook for 4 minutes, or until the broccoli is crisp-tender. Drain the broccoli and season it with salt and pepper. Divide the broccoli among 4 serving plates.

Slice the chicken breasts and serve with the broccoli.

Note

If you stuff and crumb the chicken breasts a day in advance, you can have this on the table in about 20 minutes. (Put them on a plate, cover with plastic wrap, and refrigerate.)

brazilian-style chicken with okra

I think a lot of people must have had a bad first experience with okra, because so many seem reluctant to eat it. And truthfully, it is one of those foods that's great when done well—to me it has a delicious taste not unlike asparagus—and can be terrible if overcooked. Okra adds a distinctive texture and delicate flavor to this surprisingly refined stew, which gets a bit of zing from jalapeños but is not overpoweringly spicy.

Serves 4

4 chicken drumsticks

4 chicken thighs

Salt and freshly ground black pepper

2 tablespoons olive oil

1 onion, thinly sliced

1 red bell pepper, seeded and thinly sliced

1 yellow bell pepper, seeded and thinly sliced

2 plum tomatoes, thinly sliced

1 or 2 jalapeños, finely chopped

1 garlic clove, finely chopped

1 cup dry white wine

10 fresh okra pods, thinly sliced on the diagonal

Score the skin on the chicken drumsticks and thighs with a sharp knife. Sprinkle the chicken all over with salt and black pepper.

Place a large heavy frying pan over medium-high heat. Drizzle the oil into the hot pan and add the chicken, skin side down. Cook for 5 minutes, or until the skin is golden brown. Then turn the chicken over and cook the second side for about 5 minutes, or until golden brown. Transfer the chicken pieces to a plate and drain all but 1 tablespoon of the oil from the pan. (The chicken will be golden brown on the outside but will not be cooked through at this point.)

Add the onions to the pan and sauté for 2 minutes. Add the bell peppers, tomatoes, jalapeños, and garlic, and sauté for 4 minutes, or until the peppers have softened slightly. Season the vegetables with salt and pepper to taste. Stir in the wine, and return the chicken to the pan. Cover and simmer for 10 minutes.

Stir the okra into the stew, cover the pan, and cook for 10 minutes, or until the chicken is cooked through. Serve and smile!

skirt steaks marinated in red wine and juniper berries with roasted beets

Skirt steak has a delicious intense flavor but it can be a bit chewy. There are a couple of ways you can sort this out: first, marinating helps to tenderize it, and second, slicing it thin makes it less tough. This is one instance where it's best to carve the meat for your guests before you serve it, and it's super-important to let the meat rest before you carve it; otherwise all the juices will be lost and the meat will toughen up.

Serves 4

Four 8-ounce skirt steaks

2 cups dry red wine

1 tablespoon dried juniper berries, crushed

8 baby beets (about 1$\frac{1}{2}$ inches in diameter), scrubbed, stems trimmed, beets halved lengthwise

2 teaspoons plus 1 tablespoon olive oil

Salt and freshly ground black pepper

$\frac{1}{3}$ cup red wine vinegar

Combine the skirt steaks, 1$\frac{1}{2}$ cups of the red wine, and the juniper berries in a 13 x 9-inch baking dish. Cover and refrigerate for 6 to 8 hours.

Heat a charcoal grill to medium-high or set out a grill pan. Preheat the oven to 350°F.

Place the beets in a medium-size ovenproof sauté pan and toss with the 2 teaspoons olive oil to coat. Arrange the beets, cut side down, in a single layer in the pan. Sprinkle with salt and pepper. Place the pan over medium heat for 2 minutes. Then transfer the pan to the oven and roast the beets for 10 minutes. Turn the beets over and continue roasting for 10 minutes longer, or until they are tender. Remove the beets from the oven and set the pan over medium-high heat. Add the remaining $\frac{1}{2}$ cup red wine and the vinegar to the hot pan and simmer for 8 minutes, or until the liquids are reduced to a glaze and coat the beets.

Meanwhile, if you are using a grill pan, heat it over high heat for 4 to 5 minutes. Remove the steaks from the marinade and pat them dry with paper towels. Discard the marinade. Sprinkle the steaks with salt and pepper, and rub them with the remaining 1 tablespoon olive oil. Grill over very hot coals or in the hot grill pan for about 2 minutes on each side for medium-rare. Transfer the steaks to a cutting board and let them rest for 2 to 3 minutes.

Cut the steaks across the grain into thin slices, and divide the slices evenly among 4 serving plates. Divide the beets among the plates. Drizzle the accumulated juices from the steaks over the steaks and beets, and serve.

t-bone steaks with chipotle-cilantro butter

Who hasn't woken up with an overwhelming craving for a nice, big steak, the kind that makes you think of a great old-school steak house? This will satisfy that craving big time. Trust me, ladies: If you want to make your man smile, cook him one of these.

Serves 4

8 tablespoons (1 stick) butter, at room temperature

2 tablespoons chopped canned chipotle chiles in adobo

2 tablespoons chopped fresh cilantro

1 tablespoon tequila

Four 10- to 12-ounce T-bone steaks

Salt and freshly ground black pepper

Mix the butter, chiles, cilantro, and tequila in a bowl to blend. Lay a sheet of plastic wrap on a work surface. Spoon the chile butter onto the center of the plastic wrap and roll it into a cylinder. Refrigerate for at least 2 to 3 hours or overnight.

Heat a barbecue grill to medium-high, or preheat a grill pan over medium-high heat. Sprinkle the steaks with salt and black pepper. Grill the steaks on one side for 5 minutes.

Meanwhile, cut the chile-butter log crosswise into 8 slices, and set aside.

Turn the steaks over and top each steak with 2 butter slices. Continue grilling for 5 minutes for medium-rare, or until the butter begins to melt. Transfer the steaks to plates, and serve.

veal cutlet coated in an
aged jack cheese crust

Aged Jack cheese, also called Dry Jack, has a firm texture and a sharp, slightly nutty flavor much like Parmesan cheese, which makes a good substitute. When you gently pan-fry this thin piece of veal, the cheese melts and forms a delicious golden crust.

Serves 4

Vinaigrette

2 tablespoons honey

2 tablespoons white wine vinegar

2 tablespoons finely chopped fresh chives

1 tablespoon Dijon mustard

2 tablespoons extra-virgin olive oil

Salt and freshly ground black pepper

Veal

1¼ cups fresh breadcrumbs

1⅓ cups finely grated aged Jack cheese

2 large eggs

All-purpose flour, for dredging

4 veal cutlets
(about 5 ounces each)

Salt and freshly ground black pepper

4 tablespoons (½ stick) butter

2 tablespoons extra-virgin olive oil

Salad

4 cups (lightly packed) fresh baby spinach leaves

Whisk the honey, vinegar, chives, and Dijon mustard in a medium bowl to blend. Slowly add the oil while constantly whisking. Season the vinaigrette to taste with salt and pepper, and set it aside.

To prepare the veal: Mix the breadcrumbs and Jack cheese together in a pie plate. Lightly whisk the eggs in another pie plate to blend. Place the flour in a third pie plate. Sprinkle the veal cutlets generously with salt and pepper on both sides. Dip the veal cutlets into the flour to coat lightly, then into the eggs, and finally into the breadcrumb mixture, patting the crumb mixture to make it adhere.

Melt 2 tablespoons of the butter with 1 tablespoon of the oil in each of 2 large nonstick frying pans over medium-high heat. Add 2 veal cutlets to each pan and cook for 3 minutes on each side, or until golden brown and just cooked through. Transfer the cooked veal to a paper-towel-lined plate to absorb any excess oil and butter. Cut the veal pieces in half.

In a large bowl, toss the spinach leaves with enough vinaigrette to coat. Mound the spinach on 4 plates. Arrange the veal on the spinach, and serve.

Note
To make the breadcrumbs, just tear sourdough bread into large chunks and grind them in a food processor until crumbs form.

pan-fried pork wrapped in
prosciutto with sage
and capers

Pork wrapped in pork—what could be wrong with that? Saltimbocca, the Italian dish on which this is based, is usually made with veal, but pork works just as well and is far easier to get your hands on. The prosciutto turns super-crispy and all the salty flavors really taste delicious with the sweet pork. Best of all, you can have this on the table in less than twenty minutes.

Serves 4

Four 6-ounce pork cutlets
(½ inch thick)

Freshly ground black pepper

4 thin slices prosciutto

4 tablespoons olive oil

12 fresh sage leaves

2 tablespoons drained capers

1 tablespoon butter

1 lemon

6 ounces fresh baby
spinach leaves

Salt

Preheat the oven to 300°F.

Sprinkle the pork cutlets with black pepper, and wrap a slice of prosciutto around the center of each cutlet. Place a large nonstick sauté pan over high heat. Drizzle 1 tablespoon of the oil into the hot pan, and add 2 prosciutto-wrapped pork cutlets. Cook for 2 minutes on each side, or until the pork is golden brown and cooked through. Transfer the pork to a rimmed baking sheet and place in the oven to keep warm. Repeat with the remaining 2 prosciutto-wrapped pork cutlets. Do not wipe out the sauté pan.

Immediately add 1 tablespoon oil and the sage leaves to the sauté pan, and cook for 1 minute. Remove the pan from the heat, and add the capers and butter. Grate the lemon zest over the capers. Swirl the pan to melt the butter and combine the flavors. Cut the lemon in half and squeeze the juice through a strainer into the caper mixture. Stir in any juices that have accumulated around the pork. Keep the sauce warm.

Heat the remaining 1 tablespoon oil in a separate large sauté pan over medium-high heat. Add the spinach and sprinkle with salt and pepper. Sauté for 2 minutes, or just until the spinach wilts. Divide the spinach among 4 serving plates, and place a pork cutlet on each mound of spinach. Pour the caper sauce over the pork cutlets, and serve.

roasted rack of lamb
with parsley, dijon, and chives

As a kid, when I came home and found my mum was making rack of lamb, I always said *yes!*—and I still love it. To me, lamb racks have the perfect ratio of meat to fat to bone, which gives them an absolutely delicious flavor. Considering how hassle-free they are to cook, they are a very easy way to make a meal seem special. This is lovely served with the Provençal Ratatouille (page 211).

Serves 4

Two 1¼- to 1½-pound racks of lamb (each with 8 bones), well trimmed

Salt and freshly ground black pepper

2 tablespoons extra-virgin olive oil

½ cup finely chopped fresh flat-leaf parsley

½ cup finely chopped fresh chives

3 tablespoons Dijon mustard

Preheat the oven to 450°F. Place a large heavy frying pan over high heat. Sprinkle the lamb with salt and pepper. Drizzle 1 tablespoon of the oil into the hot pan and place 1 lamb rack in the pan, meat side down. Sear for about 2 minutes per side, or until golden brown on both sides. Transfer the lamb rack to a heavy baking sheet, meat side up. Repeat with the second lamb rack.

When both racks have been browned, transfer the baking sheet to the oven and roast the lamb for 15 minutes, or until a meat thermometer inserted into the center of one end registers 120°F for medium-rare. Transfer the lamb to a platter to rest for 10 minutes.

Sprinkle the parsley and chives evenly over a plate. Spread the Dijon mustard over the meat side of the lamb racks, and then press the mustard-coated side of the lamb firmly into the herbs, creating a green herb crust. Carve the lamb between the bones into individual chops. Place the chops on 4 serving plates, drizzle with the remaining 1 tablespoon oil and any accumulated juices from the lamb and the pan, and serve.

chapter six
crowd-pleasers

I get so much pleasure out of spending time with the special people in my world, and there's no more obvious way to bring people together than to invite them around for a bite to eat. As much as I love cooking, when my friends and family are around, they take priority—but I would never want them to miss out on a fantastic meal, so I've pulled together these recipes to show you how you can be the host with the most and have friends thinking that you have a team of chefs out back, preparing the meal while you are busy entertaining.

When you are entertaining a crowd, there are two ways to go: You can choose something that cooks slowly, like my braised lamb shanks or Spinach and Ricotta Cannelloni, or you can opt for something where the preparation is done well in advance and quickly put together before serving, like my Chili Crab or Seafood Cooked in White Wine, Lemon, and Parsley.

You'll be amazed at what a little bit of imagination and preparation will achieve. By choosing your favorite tunes and lighting a few candles, you can set the mood instantly. I love to have a fun cocktail ready so that when people arrive, they are greeted with a welcome drink: They take a sip and feel like my home is theirs. While dinner is slowly bubbling away in the kitchen, shooting out inviting wafts of delicious-ness, your party has already begun.

When it comes to serving the food, I usually keep things family-style, crowding the dining table with all sorts of delicious sides and food designed to share. There's noth-ing cozier than watching friends interact, passing and sharing food around the table. Just hope that you're not sitting next to me, as even the food on your plate isn't safe!

cheese fondue

There is nothing like a good fondue night, starting with cheese and ending with chocolate! Don't forget the rule: If you drop something in the pot, it's a kiss for the person next to you. In Switzerland, blending different cheeses for fondue is very common because each variety lends a unique flavor and texture. Here, I've combined Gruyère, the most traditional choice, with Raclette cheese, which has a more pronounced flavor and a smoother texture. For a sharp, tangy flavor, I like to add just a touch of blue cheese.

Serves 4

Fondue

6 tablespoons (¾ stick) butter

3 tablespoons all-purpose flour

¼ cup Kirsch
(clear cherry brandy)

1½ cups whole milk

6 ounces Gruyère cheese, cubed

3 ounces Raclette
cheese, cubed

3 ounces creamy blue cheese
or Fontina cheese, cubed

Freshly grated nutmeg, to taste

Accompaniments

2 Yukon Gold potatoes,
quartered

3 cups broccoli florets

1 loaf crusty French bread,
torn into bite-size pieces

1 yellow squash, cut into sticks

1 zucchini, cut into sticks

½ English cucumber,
cut into sticks

4 scallions, quartered crosswise

Melt the butter in a large heavy saucepan over medium-low heat. Add the flour and whisk for 1 minute or until the mixture is smooth and bubbling. Slowly whisk in the Kirsch; then whisk in the milk. Bring the sauce to a gentle simmer. Gradually add the cheeses, stirring until all the cheese has melted and the mixture is smooth (you may need to add a little more milk if the mixture becomes too thick). Season with nutmeg to taste. Keep warm.

Bring about 1 inch of water to a simmer in the bottom of a vegetable steamer. Add the potatoes to the steamer basket, cover, and steam until they are tender, about 10 minutes. Then transfer the potatoes to a platter. Next, steam the broccoli florets until crisp-tender, about 2 minutes. Arrange them alongside the potatoes.

Transfer the fondue to a fondue pot and place it over a gel-fuel or canned-heat (Sterno) burner to keep it warm. Arrange the bread, yellow squash, zucchini, cucumber, and scallions alongside the broccoli and potatoes on the platter. Serve the bread and vegetables with the fondue, allowing guests to skewer them with a fork and dip them into the molten cheese.

prosciutto and portobello mushroom pizza

I love to host pizza nights. You can prepare all the toppings well ahead, and then when your guests arrive, get them to try spinning some dough. It's a lot of fun. Using a pizza stone helps form a deliciously crunchy crust, but if you don't have one, just assemble and bake each pizza on the back of a heavy baking sheet.

Makes 2 pizzas; serves 2 to 4

1 portobello mushroom, stemmed

3 teaspoons extra-virgin olive oil

Salt and freshly ground black pepper

All-purpose flour, for dusting

Two 8-ounce balls store-bought pizza dough

Yellow cornmeal, for dusting

2/3 cup store-bought marinara sauce

6 marinated quartered artichoke hearts, each cut in half lengthwise

6 ounces mozzarella cheese, grated (about 1 cup)

4 very thin slices prosciutto

1/2 cup (lightly packed) fresh arugula

Place a large baking stone on the bottom shelf in the oven, and preheat the oven to 450°F.

Place the portobello mushroom on a heavy baking sheet and drizzle with 1 teaspoon of the oil. Bake for about 10 minutes, or until the mushroom is tender and its juices are released. Let the mushroom cool, and then cut it into 3/4-inch slices. Combine the mushroom strips and any accumulated juices in a bowl. Season the mushroom strips with salt and pepper to taste, and set aside.

Lightly dust a work surface with flour, and press 1 ball of pizza dough into a thin round disk that is about 9 inches in diameter. Lightly dust a pizza paddle with cornmeal, and place the dough on the pizza paddle. Spread 1/3 cup of the marinara sauce over the dough in a thin layer, leaving a 1/2-inch border around the edge. Arrange half of the mushroom strips and half of the artichokes over the pizza. Sprinkle with half of the cheese. Immediately transfer the pizza from the paddle to the hot baking stone, and bake for about 10 minutes, or until the bottom is crisp and deep golden brown and the cheese has melted and become pale golden on top. Using the pizza paddle, remove the pizza from the stone and transfer it to a cutting board. Repeat with the remaining dough, marinara sauce, mushrooms, artichokes, and cheese.

Drape the prosciutto over the pizzas and scatter the arugula on top. Drizzle with the remaining 2 teaspoons oil. Cut each pizza into 4 or 6 slices, and serve. Turn the oven off, leaving the baking stone in the oven to cool slowly.

spinach and ricotta cannelloni

Truthfully, this is a bit more labor-intensive than something like lasagna, but it's definitely worth it. (If you have kids, let them help you with the filling; they really enjoy it.) Try this dish when you have vegetarians on the guest list (or suspect you may); it's so satisfying that even the carnivores won't feel cheated. When I make the tomato and béchamel sauces, I always make a double batch and freeze half for next time.

Serves 4

Tomato sauce

2 tablespoons olive oil

1 shallot, finely chopped

2 garlic cloves, minced

2 large sprigs fresh thyme

1 bay leaf

½ cup dry white wine

1½ pounds ripe heirloom or plum tomatoes, coarsely chopped

Salt and freshly ground black pepper

Béchamel sauce

4 tablespoons (½ stick) butter

⅓ cup all-purpose flour

3 cups whole milk

Freshly grated nutmeg, to taste

Salt and freshly ground black pepper

Spinach and ricotta filling

1 tablespoon oil

1 bunch fresh baby spinach, stemmed

1 pound fresh ricotta cheese

1 bunch fresh basil, coarsely chopped

Salt and freshly ground black pepper

Cannelloni

Eight 5-inch square fresh pasta sheets

⅓ cup freshly grated Parmesan cheese

To make the tomato sauce: Heat the oil in a large heavy saucepan over medium-high heat. Add the shallots and garlic, and sauté for 1 to 2 minutes, or until tender. Add the thyme sprigs and bay leaf. Add the wine and tomatoes and bring to a simmer. Simmer gently, uncovered, over medium-low heat for 1½ hours, or until the tomatoes break down to form a chunky sauce (you may need to add a little water during the cooking process if the sauce thickens too much). Season the sauce with salt and pepper to taste. Remove the thyme sprigs and bay leaf. Set aside.

To make the béchamel sauce: Melt the butter in a medium-size heavy saucepan over medium-low heat. Add the flour and stir for 3 minutes, or until thick. Slowly add the milk and stir constantly until the sauce is smooth. Bring the sauce to a simmer and cook for 5 minutes, or until the sauce is thick

and smooth. Season to taste with a little nutmeg, salt, and pepper. Set aside.

To make the spinach and ricotta filling: Heat the oil in a large sauté pan over medium heat. Add the spinach and sauté for 2 minutes, or until wilted. Transfer the wilted spinach to a colander to drain off the excess liquid. Once the spinach is cool enough to handle, squeeze it to remove any excess moisture. Coarsely chop the spinach, place it in a bowl, and mix it with the ricotta and basil. Season the spinach mixture with salt and pepper to taste, and set it aside.

To assemble the cannelloni: Preheat the oven to 425°F. Bring a large pot of salted water to a boil over high heat. Working in batches, add the pasta sheets to the boiling water and cook for 1 to 2 minutes, or until they soften slightly. Using tongs, transfer the pasta sheets to a baking sheet, arranging them in a single layer, and let them cool slightly.

Spoon the tomato sauce into a 13 x 9 x 2-inch baking dish. Lay 1 pasta sheet on a work surface. Spoon about ⅓ cup of the spinach filling over one end of the pasta sheet, and roll the pasta sheet around the filling. Place the cannelloni, seam side down, on the tomato sauce. Repeat with the remaining pasta sheets and spinach filling, forming 8 cannelloni total. Top with a thick layer of the béchamel sauce, coating the cannelloni completely. Sprinkle with the Parmesan cheese. Bake for 30 minutes, or until the sauce is bubbling and the cannelloni are heated through. Let the cannelloni stand for 10 minutes, and then serve.

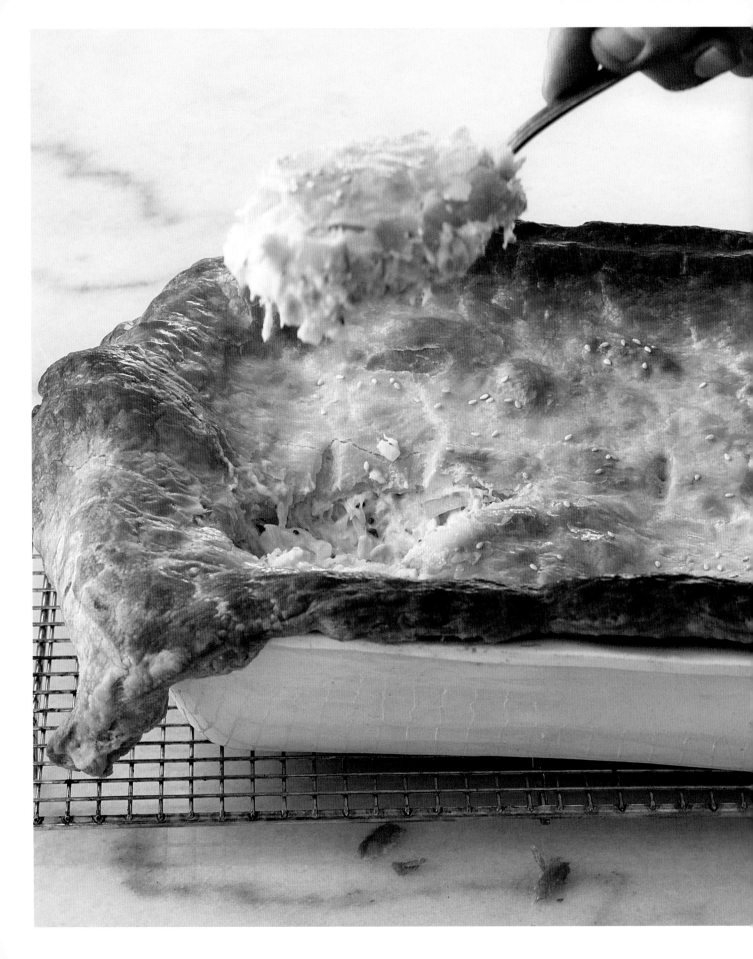

chicken and leek pie

This creamy pie sets such a comfortable atmosphere. There's nothing like the aroma of pastry baking—you can smell it the moment you walk into the house. Best of all, you can get all the work out of the way in advance and let it bake as your guests are arriving. Serve it with a nice seasonal salad.

Serves 4

3 whole corn-fed-chicken legs (thigh and drumstick)

Salt and freshly ground black pepper

1 teaspoon olive oil

2 tablespoons (¼ stick) butter

1 onion, finely diced

1 leek (white and pale green parts only), cut in half lengthwise, then cut into ½-inch strips

1 tablespoon coarse-grain mustard

¼ cup all-purpose flour

1 cup chicken stock

¾ cup plus 1 tablespoon whole milk

¼ cup heavy cream

2 tablespoons finely chopped fresh tarragon

1 sheet frozen puff pastry, thawed

1 large egg

Sesame seeds, for garnish

Preheat the oven to 400°F. Sprinkle the chicken legs with salt and pepper and drizzle with the olive oil. Place the chicken legs on a large, heavy, rimmed baking sheet and roast for 15 minutes. Turn the chicken legs over and continue roasting for 15 minutes, or until they are golden brown and cooked through. Set them aside to cool slightly, and reduce the oven temperature to 375°F. Reserve the pan drippings on the baking sheet.

When the chicken legs are cool enough to handle, shred the meat into large chunks and place it in a bowl. Discard the sinew, bones, and skin.

Melt the butter in a large heavy saucepan over medium heat. Add the onions and leeks and sauté for 5 minutes, or just until tender but not browned. Stir in the mustard, then the flour, and cook over low heat for 2 minutes, stirring constantly. Slowly whisk in the chicken broth, the ¾ cup milk, the cream, and the reserved pan drippings. Simmer, stirring occasionally, for 5 minutes, or until the sauce thickens. Stir in the shredded chicken and the tarragon, and season to taste with salt and pepper. Set the mixture aside to cool, and then refrigerate it to cool completely.

To assemble the pie: Spoon the chicken mixture into a 1½-quart baking dish. Roll out the sheet of puff pastry to form an 11-inch square. Drape the puff pastry over the chicken mixture and press it against the rim of the baking dish to seal. Cut slits into the pastry to allow steam to escape. Mix the egg and the remaining 1 tablespoon milk in a small bowl to blend. Brush the pastry with the egg mixture, and garnish with sesame seeds. Set the pie on a heavy baking sheet and bake for 50 minutes, or until the pastry is golden brown. Set it aside for 30 minutes to cool slightly before serving.

seafood cooked in white wine, lemon, and parsley

All the preparation for this dish can be done well in advance. It cooks in only minutes and can be cooked outside over a hot grill or over an open fire on the beach—even over a campfire. If you've got a fire pit with a grill insert, this will work beautifully. Don't worry too much about what kind of seafood to use—it's delicious with whatever you can get your hands on.

Serves 4

About 8 tablespoons extra-virgin olive oil

2 shallots, finely diced

2 jalapeños, seeded and finely chopped

4 garlic cloves, finely chopped

2 sprigs fresh thyme

2 bay leaves

2 lobster tails, split lengthwise

1 pound colossal shrimp in the shells

2 pounds small fresh clams, scrubbed

2 pounds fresh mussels, scrubbed and debearded (see Note, page 139)

$1/2$ cup dry white wine

3 tablespoons coarsely chopped fresh flat-leaf parsley

2 tablespoons extra-fine capers

Grated zest and juice of 1 lemon

Sea salt and freshly ground black pepper

Country-style crusty bread, for serving

Heat 2 tablespoons of the oil in a large heavy sauté pan over medium heat. Add the shallots and jalapeños, and sauté for 30 seconds. Stir in the garlic, thyme sprigs, and bay leaves. Add the lobster and shrimp, toss gently to coat, and cook for 2 minutes. Add the clams and cook for about 2 minutes. Add the mussels and cook for about 5 minutes, or until the mussels and clams begin to open. Pour in the wine and immediately cover the pan. Cook for $1 1/2$ minutes, or until the clams and mussels open completely. (Discard any that do not open.) Add the parsley, capers, and lemon zest and juice, and toss to combine. Remove the pan from the heat and stir in the remaining 5 tablespoons extra-virgin olive oil, or to taste. Season with salt and black pepper. Discard the bay leaves and thyme sprigs.

Divide the seafood mixture among 4 serving bowls. Serve with crusty bread.

paella with shrimp, mussels, clams, and scallops

Don't think of this as a rice dish; think of it as a seafood dish with a little bit of rice for accompaniment. Communal dishes like this one, which encourage everyone to lean over the table and serve themselves, set the kind of tone I like best for entertaining. Whip up a batch of sangria and a simple salad, and make a Spanish evening of it. And seeing as it goes into the oven thirty-five minutes before serving, there is nothing for you to do except enjoy your company.

Serves 4

¼ cup olive oil

3 shallots, finely chopped

3 garlic cloves, minced

3 sprigs fresh thyme

2 bay leaves

2 pinches saffron threads

2 cups long-grain white rice

½ cup dry white wine

1 teaspoon salt

4 cups chicken broth, warmed

1 tomato, seeded and diced

8 mussels, scrubbed and debearded (see Note, page 139)

8 Manila or littleneck clams, scrubbed

4 colossal shrimp in the shell, split open down the back and deveined with shells left intact

4 sea scallops

1 tablespoon coarsely chopped fresh flat-leaf parsley

1 tablespoon extra-virgin olive oil

1 lemon, halved

Preheat the oven to 425°F. Heat the olive oil in a 12-inch paella pan or ovenproof skillet over medium heat. Add the shallots and sauté for 2 minutes. Add the garlic, thyme sprigs, and bay leaves, and sauté for about 1 minute, or until the shallots are tender and translucent. Sprinkle the saffron over the shallot mixture and sauté for 1 minute. Add the rice and stir for 2 minutes, or until the pan is quite dry and the rice is coated with oil. Stir in the wine and salt, and then the warm chicken stock. Stir the rice to distribute it evenly in the pan. Bring to a simmer over high heat, and then remove the pan from the heat. Sprinkle the tomatoes over the rice mixture. Carefully transfer the pan to the oven and bake the paella, uncovered, for about 20 minutes, or until the rice is almost tender.

Nestle the mussels, clams, shrimp, and scallops into the paella and continue baking for 15 minutes, or until the rice is tender and the seafood is just cooked. Discard any mussels and clams that do not open, as well as the bay leaves and thyme sprigs.

Sprinkle with the chopped parsley and drizzle with the extra-virgin olive oil. Squeeze the lemon juice over the paella, and serve.

chili crab

This spicy crab dinner is guaranteed to make a mess, so cover the table with old newspapers, set out finger bowls, and line up some cold beers. Buying fresh crabs may be a bit of a production, depending on where you live, and you may need to preorder them. Big beautiful Dungeness crabs from the West Coast are my preference, but you can substitute whatever kind of live crabs are available near you, increasing the quantity accordingly if your local variety is smaller in size. Either way, oh, what a party.

Serves 4

Two 2-pound live Dungeness crabs (see Note)

1 tablespoon olive oil

2 shallots, finely diced

3 garlic cloves, minced

1 small red jalapeño, finely chopped

1 tablespoon finely chopped or grated peeled fresh ginger

⅓ cup Chinese Shaoxing rice wine or dry sherry

3 tablespoons rice vinegar

2 tablespoons reduced-sodium soy sauce

1 tablespoon Thai-style sweet chili sauce

1 tablespoon sugar

Fresh cilantro sprigs, for garnish

Note
If you can only find whole crabs that are already cooked, just skip the first step of plunging them in boiling water to cook them.

To prepare the crabs: To kill the crabs humanely, place them in the freezer for 2 hours. Meanwhile, bring a large pot of water to a boil over high heat. Once the crabs are no longer moving, plunge them into the boiling water for about 60 seconds or just until the shells begin to turn red. Remove the crabs from the water and set them on a baking sheet to cool.

Remove the legs and claws and lightly tap the body shell with the back of a knife to crack it. Remove the top shell from each crab body and clean the insides with your fingers. Using a large sharp knife, cut the main body of each crab into 4 pieces.

Place a large wok over high heat. When it is hot, drizzle the oil into the wok. Add the shallots, garlic, jalapeño, and ginger, and stir for 30 seconds, or until fragrant. Add all the crab pieces, including the claws, and stir for 5 minutes. Add the Chinese rice wine and stir for 3 minutes, or until the wine is reduced by half.

Combine the vinegar, soy sauce, sweet chili sauce, and sugar in a small bowl, and drizzle the mixture over the crabs. Toss to combine and cook for 2 minutes, or until the crab meat is cooked through. Transfer the crab pieces to a serving platter and spoon the sauce over them. Garnish with cilantro sprigs, and serve.

tandoori platter

Despite their somewhat fierce appearance, tandoori-roasted foods are actually rather mildly flavored. A traditional tandoori oven gets super-hot, so don't be scared to cook the chicken at a high temperature; the marinade will keep it nice and moist. Tandoori paste is a flavorful mixture of Indian spices and aromatics, such as ginger, coriander, cumin, turmeric, and tamarind. You'll find it at Indian markets and in the ethnic foods section of some supermarkets. This is another meal that lends itself to a theme night: Put on some Bollywood music, buy some good chutneys and Indian breads, and serve mango lassis, a smooth yogurt drink. See the tandoori photograph on page 171.

Serves 4

½ cup tandoori paste

⅓ cup fresh lemon juice

1¼ cups plain yogurt

2 Cornish game hens
(each about 1½ pounds),
split lengthwise and
backbone removed

Salt

12 colossal shrimp in the shell,
split open down the back and
deveined, with shells intact

1 cucumber, peeled, seeded,
and finely chopped

Freshly ground black pepper

½ head iceberg lettuce,
very thinly sliced (optional)

Lemon wedges, for garnish

Fresh cilantro sprigs, for garnish

Store-bought mango chutney,
for serving

Store-bought naan bread,
for serving

Whisk the tandoori paste, lemon juice, and ¼ cup of the yogurt in a 13 x 9 x 2-inch baking dish to blend. Using a large sharp knife, score the skin of the game hens. Sprinkle the hen halves with salt. Add the hen halves to the tandoori marinade and rub the marinade all over them. Cover and refrigerate for 1 hour.

Add the shrimp to the same dish and rub them all over with the marinade. Continue to marinate the hen halves and shrimp for 45 minutes.

Preheat the oven to 500°F. Line a large, heavy, rimmed baking sheet with foil. Place a wire rack on the baking sheet. Set the hen halves, skin side up, on the rack. Roast the hen halves until they are almost cooked through, about 20 minutes. Arrange the shrimp on the rack alongside the hen halves and roast until the hen halves and the shrimp are cooked through and golden brown, about 10 minutes.

Meanwhile, stir the cucumber and the remaining 1 cup yogurt together in a bowl. Season with salt and pepper to taste, and reserve.

Sprinkle the lettuce on a platter, if desired. Arrange the hen halves and shrimp atop the lettuce. Garnish with lemon wedges and cilantro sprigs. Serve with the raita, mango chutney, and naan bread.

indian lamb curry

In London a good curry is a way of life, and having lived there for ten years, I became very accustomed to being invited over to a pal's home for a nice afternoon curry. Despite the long list of spices, curries are actually very simple to make, and if you are missing one or two spices, it's not the end of the world. I generally start my curry in the morning and let it simmer through the day so that when guests arrive, everything is done. Make a double batch and freeze half for another time. This curry is quite mild, so if you like it hot, add a little more cayenne pepper.

Serves 4

1 tablespoon cumin seeds

10 cardamom pods

1 teaspoon fennel seeds

1 teaspoon cayenne pepper

1 teaspoon curry powder

1 teaspoon ground turmeric

4 tablespoons vegetable oil

1 onion, thinly sliced

3 garlic cloves, finely chopped

1 tablespoon finely chopped peeled fresh ginger

2 pounds well-trimmed boneless leg of lamb, cut into 1½-inch cubes

Salt

2 tomatoes, finely diced

1 russet potato, peeled and cut into 1-inch cubes

2 carrots, peeled and cut into 1-inch chunks

1 celery stalk, cut crosswise into thick slices

⅔ cup shelled fresh peas or thawed frozen peas

½ cup unsweetened coconut milk

2 cups fresh spinach leaves

Steamed basmati rice, for serving

Stir the cumin seeds, cardamom pods, and fennel seeds in a medium-size heavy skillet over medium heat for about 8 minutes, or until fragrant and toasted. Let the spices cool. Then crush the spices with a mortar and pestle or in a spice grinder until they form a powder. Stir in the cayenne pepper, curry powder, and turmeric.

Heat 2 tablespoons of the oil in a large heavy pot over medium-high heat. Add the onion slices and sauté until they become pale golden, about 8 minutes. Add the garlic and ginger, and sauté for 2 minutes, or until tender. Add the spice mixture and sauté for 2 minutes. Transfer the onion mixture to a bowl.

Heat the remaining 2 tablespoons oil in the same pot over high heat. Sprinkle the lamb with salt. Add the lamb to the hot oil and cook until browned on all sides, about 10 minutes. Return the onion mixture to the pot. Stir in the tomatoes and 4 cups water. Bring the liquid to a simmer and continue to simmer uncovered over medium-low heat, stirring occasionally, for 1 hour.

Add the potatoes, carrots, and celery to the pot. If necessary, add more water to cover the meat and vegetables. Cook, stirring occasionally, until the vegetables are almost tender, about 30 minutes. Then add the peas, season with salt, and cook for 5 minutes. Stir in the coconut milk and simmer for 5 minutes, or until the vegetables and meat are tender and the sauce has thickened slightly. Add the spinach and stir for about 2 minutes, or until it wilts. Serve with hot basmati rice.

brisket stew with fall vegetables

Brisket is one of the toughest cuts of beef, but it is inexpensive and full of flavor. By slowly stewing the brisket in red wine and stock, you end up with a dish with incredible flavor, and meat so tender that it falls apart. Serve this with rice or potatoes.

Serves 4

1 tablespoon olive oil

2¼ pounds lean beef brisket, cut into large bite-size cubes

Salt and freshly ground black pepper

2 onions, each cut into 8 pieces

2 garlic cloves, minced

1 large sprig fresh rosemary

1 large sprig fresh thyme

1¼ cups dry red wine

2 tomatoes, coarsely chopped

3 cups beef or chicken stock

2 parsnips, peeled and cut into 1-inch pieces

1 carrot, peeled and cut into 1-inch pieces

1 turnip, peeled and cut into 1-inch pieces

½ cup shelled fresh English peas

Heat the oil in a large heavy flameproof casserole over medium-high heat until it is very hot. Sprinkle the beef with salt and pepper and, working in two batches to avoid overcrowding the pot, add the beef to the pot and cook for 6 minutes, or until the beef is browned on all sides. Transfer the beef to a bowl.

Add the onions, garlic, rosemary, and thyme to the same pot and cook for about 3 minutes, or until fragrant. Add the wine and tomatoes, stirring to scrape up the browned bits on the bottom of the pot. Simmer for 8 minutes, or until the wine has reduced by about half. Return the beef and any accumulated juices to the pot. Add the stock and bring to a gentle simmer. (The beef should be just covered with the cooking liquid.) Reduce the heat to medium-low, place a lid on the pot, and cook, simmering very gently and stirring occasionally, for 1½ hours.

Add the parsnips, carrots, and turnips to the stew, and cover the pot. Simmer gently for about 55 minutes, add the peas, and continue simmering for 5 minutes, or until the vegetables are tender and the beef is tender enough to cut with a spoon.

Using a slotted spoon, transfer the beef and vegetables to a bowl. Boil the cooking liquid over high heat for 20 minutes, or until it is reduced by half. Return the beef and vegetables to the pot and simmer gently just until they are heated through.

Spoon the beef stew onto 4 serving plates, and serve rice or potatoes alongside.

all-american barbecued baby back ribs

This is a big hit whenever there are kids around. A word of warning: Put out finger bowls and plenty of napkins! You'll want to begin preparing the ribs well in advance (even up to two days ahead) to make sure they have time to marinate.

Serves 4

Dry rub and ribs

1 teaspoon Cajun or Creole seasoning

1 teaspoon dried oregano

1 teaspoon ground cumin

1 teaspoon sweet or hot paprika

2½ pounds meaty baby back pork ribs (about 2 large racks)

Barbecue sauce

2 tablespoons unsalted butter

2 medium onions, chopped

1 small celery stalk, finely chopped

2 cups beef broth

2 cups ketchup

1 cup distilled white vinegar

¾ cup (packed) light brown sugar

¼ cup fresh lemon juice

3 tablespoons Worcestershire sauce

2 tablespoons steak sauce

1½ teaspoons chili powder

1 teaspoon paprika

1 teaspoon salt

½ teaspoon dry mustard

½ teaspoon freshly ground black pepper

1 teaspoon hot sauce

Mix the Cajun seasoning, oregano, cumin, and paprika in a small bowl to blend, and rub the mixture all over the ribs. Wrap the ribs in heavy-duty foil, encasing them completely, and refrigerate for at least 1 hour and up to 1 day.

Preheat the oven to 350°F. Place the wrapped ribs on a heavy baking sheet and bake in the foil for about 1 hour, or until the meat is very tender. Unwrap the ribs and let them cool.

Meanwhile, make the barbecue sauce: Melt the butter in a large heavy saucepan over medium heat. Add the onions and celery, and sauté for 5 minutes, or until the vegetables are tender. Mix in the beef broth and all the remaining ingredients, and bring to a boil over high heat. Then reduce the heat to medium-low and simmer, uncovered, stirring occasionally, for 1 hour, or until the sauce reduces and thickens slightly.

Coat the ribs with half of the sauce and marinate for at least 1 hour at room temperature or for up to 1 day in the refrigerator. Reserve the remaining barbecue sauce.

Preheat the oven to 350°F. Place the ribs on a foil-lined, rimmed baking sheet and roast, uncovered, basting often with some of the remaining barbecue sauce, for about 25 minutes, or until the ribs are heated through. Rewarm the remaining sauce and serve it alongside the ribs.

roast loin of pork with apple compote

If something works well, why change it? Pork and apples are one of those brilliant, classic combinations, like scallops and lemon, that just can't be improved on. Pork loin is actually quite a lean cut, so don't remove the layer of fat on the outside; it bastes the pork perfectly as it roasts and keeps it from becoming dry.

Serves 4 to 6

Pork

One 3½-pound bone-in pork loin roast (with thick layer of fat on top still intact)

2 tablespoons sea salt, preferably Maldon

2 garlic cloves, coarsely chopped

2 tablespoons fresh marjoram leaves, coarsely chopped

Apple compote

5 Fuji apples (about 1½ pounds total), peeled, cored, and each cut into 8 wedges

2 whole cloves

¾ cup Calvados (apple brandy)

2 teaspoons sugar (optional)

To prepare the pork: Position a rack on the bottom of the oven and preheat the oven to 475°F. Using a sharp knife, score the fat that covers the top of the pork. Rub the pork fat with the sea salt, garlic, and half of the marjoram leaves. Place the pork on a rack set in a heavy roasting pan. Roast for 30 minutes. Then reduce the oven temperature to 350°F and roast the pork for another 45 minutes, or until an instant-read meat thermometer registers 140°F when inserted into the center of the pork.

Remove the roasting pan from the oven and allow the pork to rest for 30 minutes before carving. Combine the pan juices from the roasting pan with the remaining marjoram leaves and set aside to keep warm.

While the pork is resting, prepare the apple compote: Combine the apples and cloves in a large heavy-based saucepan over medium to high heat, and stir for 3 minutes or until the apples just begin to soften slightly. Decrease the heat to medium-low. Add the Calvados and stir for 5 minutes, or until most of the liquid has evaporated. Cover the pan and cook the apples, stirring occasionally, for 8 minutes or until they are tender and most of the juices have evaporated. Remove the saucepan from the heat. Using a potato masher, coarsely mash the apples. If necessary, stir in the sugar to sweeten the compote slightly.

Thinly slice the pork on a cutting board, and arrange the pork slices on plates. Drizzle the pan juices, and any accumulated juices that have exuded from the pork while it was being sliced, over the pork slices. Spoon the warm apple compote alongside the pork, and serve.

slowly cooked brisket with a bbq bourbon sauce

This can be the center of a party with a soul-food theme. Add corn bread and mustard greens, and even play some blues. This is an interesting barbecue sauce; the peaches and bourbon add sweetness.

Serves 10 to 12

Dry rub

1 onion, finely chopped

¼ cup smoked paprika (pimentón)

1 tablespoon chili powder

1 tablespoon chopped fresh oregano

1 tablespoon fresh thyme leaves

1 tablespoon sugar

1 tablespoon freshly ground black pepper

3 garlic cloves, finely chopped

Brisket

8 pounds beef brisket (well marbled and with top layer of fat intact)

Stir the dry rub ingredients together in a medium bowl to blend. Rub the mixture all over the brisket. Cover the brisket with plastic wrap and refrigerate it for at least 2 hours and up to 1 day.

To make the sauce: Puree the peaches in a food processor until smooth. Pass the puree through a fine-mesh strainer into a bowl, discarding any solids, and set the puree aside.

Melt the butter in a heavy pot over medium heat. Stir in the chili powder, oregano, allspice, ginger, salt, sugar, and celery seeds. Remove the pot from the heat and add the bourbon. Return the pot to medium heat and simmer gently for 1 minute. Then stir in the peach puree, barbecue sauce, ketchup, pineapple juice, soy sauce, and Worcestershire sauce, and bring to a boil. Reduce the heat to low and simmer gently for 30 minutes or until the sauce thickens.

To cook the brisket: Preheat the oven to 300°F. Unwrap the brisket and transfer it, fat side up, to a large roasting pan. Cover the pan with foil and roast, basting occasionally with

Barbecue sauce

2 ripe peaches, pitted and coarsely chopped

4 tablespoons (½ stick) unsalted butter

1 teaspoon chili powder

1 teaspoon dried oregano

1 teaspoon ground allspice

1 teaspoon ground ginger

1 teaspoon salt

1 teaspoon sugar

¼ teaspoon celery seeds

⅓ cup bourbon

2 cups prepared barbecue sauce

1 cup ketchup

1 cup pineapple juice

2 tablespoons soy sauce

2 teaspoons Worcestershire sauce

the pan juices, for 7 hours, or until the brisket is tender. Uncover the pan and brush 1 cup of the barbecue sauce over the brisket. Continue roasting, uncovered, for 1 hour, or until the brisket is very tender.

Let the brisket rest for 30 minutes; then cut it across the grain into thin slices. Serve with the remaining barbecue sauce.

lamb shanks slowly braised
in red wine, rosemary, and thyme

Lamb shanks are a wonderful way to spoil yourself—their flavor is so rich and so decadent. I also love the fact that they spend three hours in the oven, so you can get everything else organized while they slowly work their magic. The red wine tenderizes the meat so it's nearly falling off the bone. This works well with Creamy Mascarpone and Parsley Polenta (page 224).

Serves 6

Six 1-pound lamb shanks

Salt

$\frac{1}{2}$ cup all-purpose flour

1 teaspoon sweet paprika

$\frac{1}{4}$ teaspoon cayenne pepper

5 tablespoons olive oil

1 head garlic, halved crosswise

1 onion, coarsely chopped

3 carrots, peeled: 2 coarsely chopped, 1 finely diced

3 celery stalks: 2 coarsely chopped, 1 finely diced

2 sprigs fresh rosemary

2 sprigs fresh thyme

2 bay leaves

One 14.5-ounce can diced tomatoes

8 cups lamb or beef stock

1$\frac{1}{3}$ cups dry red wine

Freshly ground black pepper

Preheat the oven to 350°F. Starting at 1 inch from the narrow end of each shank, score the meat, sinew, and fat around the bone (this will help release the meat from the bone as it cooks). Sprinkle the lamb shanks with salt. Mix the flour, paprika, and cayenne pepper in a large bowl. Set aside 3 tablespoons of the flour mixture. Coat the lamb shanks thoroughly with the remaining flour mixture.

Heat 4 tablespoons of the oil in a large wide Dutch oven over medium-high heat. Add the lamb shanks and reduce the heat to medium. Cook for 10 minutes, or until the shanks are browned on all sides. Transfer the shanks to a rimmed baking sheet.

Drizzle the remaining 1 tablespoon oil in the Dutch oven, and add the garlic and the coarsely chopped onion, carrots, and celery. Cook over medium heat for 8 minutes, or until the vegetables begin to brown. Sprinkle the reserved 3 table-spoons flour mixture over the vegetables and stir to coat.

Using the back of a large knife, gently pound the rosemary and thyme sprigs to help release their flavors. Add the rosemary, thyme, and bay leaves to the vegetable mixture. Cook for 2 minutes, or until the flour is golden brown. Stir in the tomatoes and their juices, then the stock and wine. Return the lamb shanks and any accumulated juices to the

Dutch oven. Cover, transfer it to the oven, and braise for
3 hours, or until the lamb is tender. Transfer the lamb shanks
to a baking sheet and cover them with foil to keep warm.

Place the Dutch oven over medium-high heat and simmer,
uncovered, for 20 minutes to reduce and thicken the sauce.
Carefully strain the sauce through a fine-mesh strainer into a
medium saucepan. Discard the solids from the strainer.
Skim off the fat that rises to the top of the sauce. Simmer
the sauce, uncovered, for 15 minutes, or until reduced to
4 cups. Add the finely diced carrots and celery and simmer
for 5 minutes, or until the vegetables are tender. Season the
sauce with salt and pepper to taste.

Place 1 lamb shank on each of 6 plates. Spoon the sauce
and vegetables over the lamb, and serve.

caipirinha cocktail

This is so refreshing to drink. *Cachaça,* a Brazilian liquor made from sugarcane juice, gives these cocktails their unique flavor. Put one of your guests on Caipirinha duty—they're a lot of fun to make.

Serves 4

4 limes, cut into small chunks

6 tablespoons sugar

Ice cubes, coarsely crushed

1 cup cachaça

½ cup chilled club soda

Divide the lime chunks among 4 highball glasses. Sprinkle with the sugar, dividing it equally. Crush the limes with a pestle or the handle of a wooden spoon, just enough to release the juice—don't overdo it or the drinks will be bitter. Fill the glasses with ice. Add the cachaça and stir to mix. Top off each drink with 2 tablespoons club soda, stir again, and enjoy!

sangria

Cocktails are fun to serve and to drink, but if you have a number of guests, you can get stuck making refills all night. This is the perfect solution for a lazy host (like me). Sangria isn't too heavy and it's not too strong, and you can tailor it to your crowd, substituting juice for the brandy or the Cointreau if you want to keep it light and easy. Mix up a few pitchers and encourage your guests to help themselves.

Serves 6 to 8

One 750-ml bottle light and fruity Rioja or Beaujolais wine

½ cup Cointreau (or other orange liqueur)

¼ cup brandy

2 Fuji apples, quartered, cored, and thinly sliced

1 ruby-red grapefruit, quartered and thinly sliced

2 Valencia oranges, quartered and thinly sliced

1 lemon, quartered and thinly sliced

1 lime, quartered and thinly sliced

Ice cubes

Stir all the ingredients except the ice cubes in a large pitcher. Cover and refrigerate until cold. Just before serving, stir in the ice cubes. Drink and be merry!

pomegranate martini

The beautiful vibrant color of these martinis is so festive, and the flavor is just delicious. Serve these with nibbles as people arrive.

Serves 1

Ice cubes

1/3 cup pomegranate juice

1/4 cup vodka

1 tablespoon freshly squeezed orange juice

Pomegranate seeds, for garnish

Fill a cocktail shaker halfway with ice. Add the pomegranate juice, vodka, and orange juice. Shake vigorously until the outside of the shaker becomes very cold and frosty. Strain into a chilled martini glass. Garnish with pomegranate seeds, and serve immediately.

lychee-lovers' bellini

Greeting a guest with a cocktail sets a party atmosphere far more readily than offering a beer or a glass of wine. Shown in the photograph at right, this one is special but really easy—basically just a fruit puree that is slowly added to champagne or sparkling wine. Be sure to make the fruit puree in advance so it's nice and cold when you mix up the drinks. I love the addition of Chambord, but it's also great without it. If you have leftover lychee puree, freeze it in an ice cube tray and pop a couple of cubes into a glass of vodka.

Serves 4

20 fresh whole lychees, peeled and pitted (if not available, substitute canned)

8 teaspoons Chambord (black raspberry liqueur)

2 cups chilled sparkling wine

Puree the lychees in a blender until smooth. Line a fine-mesh strainer with cheesecloth and strain the puree into a bowl, pressing on the solids in the strainer to extract as much juice as possible. Discard the solids. Chill the lychee juice until it is cold.

Pour 2 tablespoons of the lychee juice and 2 teaspoons of the Chambord into each of 4 champagne flutes. Add enough sparkling wine (about 1/2 cup) to fill each glass. Stir gently to blend, and serve.

chapter seven
sides to share

I remember how vegetables were prepared when I was a kid, and looking back now, it's no wonder I found it such a chore to eat them. It wasn't until later in life that I discovered how great vegetables could taste. Paired with the right herbs or spices, your favorite vegetable side can even eclipse the entrée to become the hero of the meal. Whether it's the sweetness of the honey-glazed heirloom carrots that you've roasted or the crunchiness of the garlic sugar snaps, these colors, flavors, and textures will steal the show, transforming an ordinary meal into something you might be served in the best restaurants. Grouping a selection of sides at the center of the table makes serving dinner that much easier—and let's face it, there's nothing more relaxing than helping yourself to as much or as little of each as you like.

asparagus with raspberry-shallot vinaigrette

Believe it or not, etiquette dictates that asparagus be eaten with your hands. Even if you choose to use a fork, keep it simple when you serve asparagus so its true flavor comes through; I think it is beautifully complemented by this warm-weather raspberry vinaigrette.

Serves 4

2 pounds (about 2 bunches) asparagus

Salt

½ cup raspberry vinegar

2 small shallots, cut into thin rings

⅓ cup grapeseed oil

1 tablespoon olive oil

1 tablespoon chopped fresh flat-leaf parsley

Freshly ground black pepper

Fill a large frying pan with salted water and bring it to a boil. Trim off the woody portion of the asparagus spears, and place the asparagus in the boiling water. Sprinkle with salt and cook for 2 minutes, or until the asparagus is crisp-tender. Drain. Submerge the asparagus in a large bowl of ice-cold water to cool it completely. Drain again, and dry the asparagus with paper towels.

In a small saucepan, combine the vinegar and shallots and bring to a simmer over medium heat. Remove the saucepan from the heat and allow to cool. Strain the vinegar into a bowl, reserving the shallots separately.

Slowly add the grapeseed oil and olive oil to the vinegar, whisking constantly to blend. Whisk in the parsley, and season the vinaigrette with salt and pepper to taste.

Arrange the asparagus on plates, and pour the vinaigrette over it. Garnish with the reserved shallots, and serve.

stir-fried sugar snaps
with garlic

These sugar snaps are so tasty and adaptable—they can be served with absolutely anything. They take only minutes to prepare, and the garlic gives them a little extra kick.

Serves 4

1 tablespoon olive oil

1 pound sugar snap peas, strings removed

2 garlic cloves, finely chopped

3 tablespoons Shaoxing rice wine (yellow rice wine)

Salt

Place a wok or a sauté pan over high heat. When it is hot, add the oil and heat until it is very hot. Add the sugar snap peas and garlic, and toss lightly for 30 seconds. Add the rice wine and salt, and stir-fry for 2 minutes, or until the sugar snap peas are bright green and crisp-tender. Transfer them to a platter and serve immediately.

provençal ratatouille

Ratatouille seems like a lot of preparation, but it doesn't have to be. Don't worry too much about how you cut up the vegetables—you can do small pieces or big chunks, whichever you prefer. Make a double batch; you'll find it tastes even better the next day.

Serves 4

3 tablespoons olive oil

2 large shallots, cut into
$\frac{1}{2}$-inch pieces

1 garlic clove, minced

$\frac{1}{2}$ eggplant, unpeeled,
cut into $\frac{1}{2}$-inch pieces

2 zucchini, cut into
$\frac{1}{2}$-inch pieces

$\frac{1}{2}$ small red bell pepper, seeded
and cut into $\frac{1}{2}$-inch pieces

$\frac{1}{2}$ small yellow bell pepper,
seeded and cut into
$\frac{1}{2}$-inch pieces

$\frac{1}{4}$ cup dry red wine

1 pound ripe plum tomatoes
(about 6), cut into $\frac{1}{2}$-inch pieces

Salt and freshly ground
black pepper

$\frac{1}{4}$ cup thinly sliced fresh
basil leaves

Place a medium saucepan over medium heat, and drizzle the oil into it. Add the shallots and garlic, and sauté for 2 minutes, or until tender. Add the eggplant, zucchini, and bell peppers and cook, stirring occasionally, for 5 minutes, or until the eggplant is tender. Add the red wine, then the tomatoes, and cook, stirring occasionally, for another 8 minutes, or until the tomatoes are soft and broken down. Season the ratatouille generously with salt and black pepper. Remove from the heat and stir in the basil. Serve warm.

curried cauliflower with cardamom and mustard

This is the obvious accompaniment to anything Indian, but I also love serving it with something simple like a bit of steak, a grilled chicken breast, or even fish, to bring some color and life to the plate. Mustard oil adds a pungent aroma and spicy flavor to this dish. It is most often used in Indian cooking and is available at Indian markets. If you can't find it, use canola oil or olive oil instead. See the photograph on page 205.

Serves 4

1 teaspoon black mustard seeds

1 teaspoon yellow mustard seeds

3 cardamom pods

1 serrano chile, seeded and minced

2 garlic cloves, minced

1 teaspoon tamarind puree

1 teaspoon ground turmeric

3 tablespoons mustard oil

1 onion, very thinly sliced

Salt

1 head cauliflower, cut into small florets

Using a mortar and pestle or a spice grinder, crush the mustard seeds and cardamom pods into a fine powder. If using a spice grinder, transfer the ground spices to a bowl. Add the chile and garlic to the spices, and crush to form a paste. Mix in the tamarind puree and turmeric. Then add ½ cup water to thin the paste and form a smooth saucelike consistency.

Heat the mustard oil in a large heavy frying pan over medium-high heat. Once the oil is almost smoking, reduce the heat to medium and add the onions. Sprinkle with some salt. Sauté for 4 minutes, or until the onions are pale golden. Add the cauliflower and fry for 6 minutes, or until lightly browned.

Drizzle the spice mixture over the cauliflower, and stir well to coat. Bring to a boil, and then reduce the heat to medium-low. Cover the pan and cook, stirring occasionally, for 12 minutes, or until the cauliflower is nearly tender. (To prevent the cauliflower from sticking to the pan as it cooks, add a little more water as needed.) Remove the lid and simmer uncovered, until the excess liquid evaporates and the mixture is dry.

grilled corn on the cob with
parsley and garlic brown butter

Everyone puts butter on corn, but browning the butter first adds a nutty flavor and transforms it into a gourmet side dish. And you still get to eat it with your hands! This adds an energetic splash of color to any plate. See the photograph on page 207.

Serves 6

8 tablespoons (1 stick) butter, at room temperature

4 garlic cloves, finely chopped

1 tablespoon coarsely chopped fresh flat-leaf parsley

Juice of 1/2 lemon

6 ears yellow corn in the husks

Salt and freshly ground black pepper

Place a small heavy saucepan over medium heat. Add the butter and cook, swirling the pan occasionally, for 5 minutes, or until the butter melts and becomes golden brown. Remove the pan from the heat and stir in the garlic. Set aside until the butter is almost cold, and then add the parsley and lemon juice. Place the butter mixture in a bowl and chill until it is cold and firm.

Fold back the husks from the corn and remove the corn silk (keeping the husks attached to the cobs). Soak the corn in a large bowl of cold water for 1 hour. Drain and pat dry.

Heat a barbecue grill to medium. Tear a few corn husks into long strips. Gather the husks at the base of each corncob and tie them with the husk strips to secure them. Spread the garlic butter all over the corn kernels, and sprinkle the corn with salt and pepper. Place the corn on the grill. Cover and cook, turning occasionally, for 12 to 15 minutes, or until the corn is soft and juicy and the husks are lightly charred.

sautéed wild mushrooms
with baby spinach

When the season for wild mushrooms comes around in the fall, I celebrate and eat them as often as I can. There are so many amazing varieties to choose from. This recipe will also work well with cremini mushrooms, which are available all year round. Use a pastry brush or a damp cloth to remove any debris from the mushrooms.

Serves 4

2 tablespoons olive oil

⅓ cup diced onion

2 garlic cloves, minced

1 pound assorted fresh wild mushrooms, such as oyster, chanterelles, morels, and black trumpet, cut into large pieces if necessary

2 ounces (about 2 cups) fresh baby spinach leaves

1 tablespoon coarsely chopped fresh flat-leaf parsley

Salt and freshly ground black pepper

Heat the oil in a large sauté pan over medium heat. Add the onions and garlic and sauté for 2 minutes, or until they soften. Add the mushrooms and sauté for 8 minutes, or until tender. Remove the pan from the heat, add the spinach and parsley, and toss until the spinach softens and becomes bright green. Season with salt and pepper to taste and serve immediately.

honey-glazed heirloom carrots
with leek and thyme

No doubt you've come across heirloom tomatoes, but when you are at your farmer's market, look for beautiful old varieties of carrots, from yellow to deep red. They glisten even more with this wonderful honey glaze.

Serves 4 to 6

3 tablespoons (3/8 stick) butter

2 bunches baby heirloom carrots (about 2 pounds total), peeled and trimmed

1 leek, white and pale green parts halved lengthwise and thinly sliced (1/2 cup)

2 shallots, thinly sliced

Leaves from 1 large sprig fresh thyme

Salt and freshly ground black pepper

2 tablespoons honey

Preheat the oven to 400°F. Melt the butter in a medium roasting pan over medium heat. Add the carrots, leeks, shallots, and thyme leaves, and toss to coat them with the butter. Sprinkle with salt and pepper, and transfer the pan to the oven. Roast, stirring occasionally, for about 15 minutes, or until the carrots and shallots are tender.

Remove the pan from the oven and place it over medium heat on the stove. Drizzle the honey over the carrots, and toss gently to coat. Season with more salt and pepper, if necessary, and serve.

acorn squash roasted with thyme

In Australia it's quite common to roast pumpkin, which I really love. This acorn squash recipe reminds me of all the good things that fall brings.

Serves 6

3 acorn squash, halved lengthwise and seeded

3 tablespoons olive oil

1 tablespoon chopped fresh thyme leaves

Salt and freshly ground black pepper, to taste

1/3 cup pure maple syrup

Preheat the oven to 450°F. Cut the squash lengthwise into 3/4- to 1-inch-wide wedges. Drizzle the oil over 2 large, heavy, rimmed baking sheets. Arrange the squash, cut side down and in a single layer, on the baking sheets. Sprinkle with the thyme, salt, and pepper. Roast for 20 minutes.

Using a metal spatula, turn the squash over and drizzle with the maple syrup. Continue roasting until the squash is tender and golden brown, about 20 minutes longer. Transfer the squash to a platter, and serve.

crispy roasted potatoes

Everybody will tell you something different about the best type of potatoes to use for roasting, but the truth is that nearly all potatoes will roast well if you apply two simple rules: Get your oven hot enough, and don't overpopulate your baking sheet with too many pieces of potato. That's all there is to it.

Serves 6

6 russet potatoes, peeled, each cut into 4 equal pieces

3 tablespoons olive oil

Salt and freshly ground black pepper

1 tablespoon chopped fresh flat-leaf parsley

Preheat the oven to 450°F. Toss the potatoes with the oil on a large, rimmed baking sheet. Then arrange the potatoes in a single layer, and sprinkle with salt and pepper to taste. Roast for 20 minutes.

Using a metal spatula, turn the potatoes over. Continue roasting until the potatoes are tender and crispy on all sides, about 20 minutes longer. Transfer the potatoes to a platter, sprinkle with the parsley, and serve.

parsley potatoes

Sometimes in life, things are best kept simple. Parsley potatoes are the perfect accompaniment to slowly cooked stews, as well as to a beautiful piece of fish, when you don't want it to be overwhelmed by anything else on the plate.

Serves 4 to 6

12 medium Yukon Gold potatoes (about 2½ pounds total), peeled

6 tablespoons (¾ stick) butter, at room temperature

¼ cup coarsely chopped fresh flat-leaf parsley

Salt and freshly ground black pepper

Bring a large pot of salted water to a boil over high heat. Add the potatoes and cook for 18 to 20 minutes or until just tender (when a skewer can be inserted into the center of the potatoes without resistance). Drain the potatoes and set them aside.

Melt the butter with the parsley in a large sauté pan over medium heat. Add the potatoes and roll them in the parsley butter to coat. Season with salt and pepper to taste, and serve.

coconut rice

This is the perfect accompaniment to any Asian dish—try it with the yummy lobster curry on page 152. Combining a bit of coconut milk with the chicken stock gives the rice richness and a creamy texture, and requires no more effort than cooking it with water.

Serves 4

1 cup basmati rice

1¼ cups chicken stock

1 cup unsweetened coconut milk

½ teaspoon salt

Unsweetened grated coconut, lightly toasted, for garnish (see Note)

Rinse the rice in a sieve under cold running water until the water runs clear. Drain.

Combine the stock, coconut milk, and salt in a large heavy saucepan over medium-high heat and bring to a near boil. Reduce the heat to low. Add the rice and stir constantly for 1 minute. Then cover the pan and simmer over low heat, without stirring, for 15 minutes or until the rice is almost tender and most of the liquid has been absorbed.

Remove the pan from the heat and let the rice stand, still covered, for 10 minutes, or until it is tender and all of the liquid has been absorbed. Lightly fluff up the rice with a fork.

Transfer the rice to bowls. Garnish with the toasted coconut, and serve.

Note

You can buy unsweetened coconut, sometimes labeled desiccated coconut, at health food stores. Better yet, shave a chunk of fresh coconut with a vegetable peeler to make shavings. Toast coconut in a dry skillet over medium heat, tossing often, until fragrant and pale golden, 4 to 5 minutes.

corn bread

I had never encountered corn bread until I came to America, and I loved it straight-away. Even when the outside is crisp and crunchy, the center is soft and delicious—a cross between a cake and a bread. It seems to me tailor-made for dipping into a fabulous sauce.

Serves 8

1 tablespoon canola oil

1½ cups stone-ground yellow cornmeal

½ cup all-purpose flour

1 tablespoon sugar

2 teaspoons baking powder

1 teaspoon baking soda

½ teaspoon salt

2 large eggs

1½ cups buttermilk

2 tablespoons (¼ stick) unsalted butter, melted

Preheat the oven to 425°F. Pour the oil into a heavy 12-inch ovenproof skillet (preferably cast iron), tilting the skillet to coat the bottom and sides.

In a large bowl, whisk together the cornmeal, flour, sugar, baking powder, baking soda, and salt, to blend. In another bowl, whisk the eggs for 60 seconds; then whisk in the buttermilk and melted butter. Stir the buttermilk mixture into the dry ingredients to blend well.

Heat the prepared skillet over medium-high heat until it is very hot. Pour the cornmeal mixture into the hot skillet, transfer it to the oven, and bake for 18 minutes, or until the corn bread is golden brown.

Remove the skillet from the oven and let it cool for 2 minutes. Then remove the corn bread from the pan, break it into chunks, and serve warm.

chapter eight
sweet dreams

saffron couscous

Saffron is the perfect partner for seafood. It's also a classic in dishes such as risotto and works really well with couscous. Don't be put off by the cost; a little goes a long way.

Serves 4

2 cups chicken broth

Large pinch of saffron threads

1 teaspoon salt

1½ cups plain couscous

¼ cup raisins

¼ cup pine nuts, toasted
(see Note)

Freshly ground black pepper

Combine the chicken broth, saffron threads, and salt in a medium saucepan, and bring to a boil over high heat. Remove the pan from the heat. Add the couscous and stir to blend. Sprinkle the raisins on top. Cover the pan tightly and let it stand until the liquid is absorbed and the couscous is tender, about 5 minutes. Fluff the couscous with a fork, and mix in the pine nuts. Season with pepper to taste, and serve.

Note

To toast pine nuts, simply place the nuts in a sauté pan and stir or toss them over medium heat so they toast evenly. They should take 4 to 5 minutes to become light golden in color.

creamy mascarpone and parsley polenta

Whenever I have a great braised dish, or a stew, or anything that's quite saucy or juicy, I think of polenta, which helps you get every bit of that delicious sauce off the plate. This is an especially mellow, rich, and tasty version.

Serves 6

5 cups chicken stock

2 cups heavy cream

2 cups whole milk

1 small sprig fresh thyme

3 garlic cloves, peeled and smashed with the side of a large knife

1 fresh bay leaf

1½ cups polenta (coarse cornmeal)

½ cup mascarpone cheese

½ cup freshly grated Parmesan cheese

2 tablespoons (¼ stick) unsalted butter

2 tablespoons chopped fresh flat-leaf parsley

Freshly grated nutmeg, to taste

Salt and freshly ground black pepper

Heat the chicken stock in a medium saucepan over medium heat just until hot. Remove the pan from the heat and cover to keep the stock warm.

Meanwhile, combine the cream, milk, thyme, garlic, and bay leaf in another medium saucepan and bring to a gentle simmer over medium-high heat.

Strain the cream mixture into a large heavy saucepan. Slowly whisk the polenta into the hot cream mixture. Whisk in the warm chicken stock. Whisk the polenta over medium heat until it boils. Reduce the heat to medium-low and simmer gently, stirring often, for 1 hour, or until the polenta has the consistency of mashed potatoes and no longer has a starchy taste.

Stir in the mascarpone cheese, Parmesan cheese, butter, and parsley. Season with nutmeg, salt, and pepper to taste, and serve.

chocolate mint martini

Who says cocktails can only be served before the meal? If you want the party to kick on after dinner, try serving this instead of a dessert, turn up the music, and get people on their feet.

Serves 2

3 tablespoons vodka

1/2 ounce semisweet chocolate, finely grated

8 ice cubes

1/2 cup half-and-half

6 tablespoons chocolate liqueur

2 tablespoons green crème de menthe

8 fresh mint leaves

Grated dark chocolate, for garnish (optional)

2 sprigs fresh mint, for garnish

Pour 1 tablespoon of the vodka onto a small plate. Place the grated semisweet chocolate on another small plate. Dip the rims of 2 martini glasses into the vodka to moisten them lightly, and then dip the rims into the grated chocolate to coat them lightly. Set aside.

Combine the ice cubes, half-and-half, chocolate liqueur, crème de menthe, remaining 2 tablespoons vodka, and mint leaves in a cocktail shaker. Shake until the mixture is icy cold and a bit frothy. Strain into the prepared martini glasses. Garnish with grated dark chocolate, if desired, and a mint sprig, and serve.

When it comes to desserts, there's no point in beating around the bush: Anything that oozes or melts, is gooey, sticky, or chocolaty, or is filled with nuts or fruit—and don't forget caramel—sends me into an utter frenzy. In other words, I have a serious sweet tooth. I've called this chapter "Sweet Dreams" because everything in it is sweet (of course), and I promise they are all dreamy.

As a young chef, I was lucky enough to work with some of Europe's best pastry chefs, who shared some incredible recipes that I've since served in some of the best restaurants around London. I've now adapted these delectable treats so that you'll find them super-easy to make for your friends and family at home.

Don't call these desserts; I'd never want to put a limitation on something sweet and say it should only be eaten after dinner. You should eat them whenever you have the desire, and without guilt. After all, in moderation, almost everything is perfectly fine to indulge in, and what is life without a little sweetness?

pots of gold

Eating this dessert is like a treasure hunt: First you dive through creamy custard; then you strike gold when you hit the caramel.

Serves 6

Caramel

1 cup sugar

Custard

1⅓ cups heavy cream

1⅓ cups whole milk

½ cup sugar

3 large eggs

3 large egg yolks

1 teaspoon pure vanilla extract

Position an oven rack in the center of the oven, and preheat the oven to 275°F. Set six 6-ounce ramekins in a roasting pan.

To make the caramel: Combine the sugar and ¼ cup water in a medium-size heavy saucepan. Stir gently over medium heat for 5 minutes, or until the sugar dissolves. Then boil without stirring, occasionally swirling the pan and brushing down the sides of the pan with a wet pastry brush to prevent sugar crystals from forming, until the syrup turns a deep golden brown, about 4 minutes. Immediately remove the saucepan from the heat and divide the syrup among the ramekins, tilting each ramekin to coat the bottom. Set them aside and allow the caramel to cool until hardened, about 10 minutes.

To make the custard: Bring the cream, milk, and sugar to a simmer in a medium-size heavy saucepan over medium heat, stirring constantly until the sugar dissolves. Remove the pan from the heat and let it cool slightly, about 5 minutes. Whisk the eggs, egg yolks, and vanilla in a large bowl to blend. Gradually whisk the cooled cream mixture into the egg mixture. Strain the custard through a fine-mesh sieve into a 4-cup measuring cup. Pour the custard over the hardened caramel in the ramekins, dividing it equally.

Transfer the roasting pan to the oven. Pour enough hot water into the pan to come halfway up the sides of the

ramekins. Bake until the outer 1-inch perimeter of the custards is softly set but the centers are still loose, about 1 hour (the custards will firm up after they are refrigerated). To test whether the custard is cooked, push a small knife into the center of one of the dishes; if the caramel rises out of the hole made by the knife, they are ready.

Remove the roasting pan from the oven, and remove the custards from the roasting pan. Refrigerate the custards overnight. (This allows time for the caramel to dissolve and form a thin sauce at the bottom.)

Arm your guests with small spoons and let them dig through the velvety custard to get to their pot of gold at the bottom.

espresso crème brûlée

Why serve both coffee and dessert? This recipe kills two birds with one stone: It's a delicious creamy dessert that also gives you a shot of espresso. Not unlike tiramisù, it provides a bit of a pick-me-up after a heavy meal.

Serves 4

1¼ cups heavy cream

⅓ cup whole milk

½ cup granulated sugar

4 shots brewed espresso

1 vanilla bean, split lengthwise

7 large egg yolks

2 tablespoons turbinado
or raw sugar

Preheat the oven to 200°F. Combine the cream, milk, granulated sugar, and espresso in a medium-size heavy saucepan. Using a spoon, scrape the seeds from the vanilla bean into the cream mixture. Whisk to blend, and then add the scraped vanilla bean to the mixture. Bring the cream mixture to a near boil over medium-high heat, stirring until the sugar and coffee dissolve. Remove from the heat and let cool for 5 minutes.

Whisk the egg yolks in a large bowl to blend. Discard the vanilla bean, and gradually whisk the warm cream mixture into the yolks. Strain the custard through a fine-mesh sieve into a 4-cup measuring cup. Place four 5-ounce custard cups or ovenproof coffee cups in a baking dish. Divide the custard among the custard cups. Place the baking dish in the oven. Fill the baking dish halfway with hot water. Bake the custards, uncovered, for 2 hours, or until the centers move only slightly when the cups are gently shaken (the custards will become firm as they cool). Remove the custards from the baking dish and let them cool. Then refrigerate the custards until cold.

Sprinkle the turbinado sugar over the custards. Using a kitchen blowtorch, wave the flame over the custards until the sugar caramelizes. Alternatively you can place the custards under a preheated broiler for 1 to 2 minutes or until the sugar has changed color to golden brown. Refrigerate the custards until the topping is cold and brittle, about 10 minutes; then serve.

chocolate pots de crème

Smooth, beautiful, chocolaty—this is so much more delightful than a mousse, which contains a lot of air. This creamy chocolate velvet can be made the day before, and can be cooked in different-size and -shape pots or cups. Use good-quality chocolate; it will really make a difference to the texture and flavor.

Serves 6

1⅔ cups heavy cream

1¼ cups whole milk

½ cup sugar

1 teaspoon pure vanilla extract

8 ounces bittersweet chocolate (70% cacao), coarsely chopped

6 large egg yolks

Position an oven rack in the center of the oven and preheat the oven to 250°F. Whisk the cream, milk, sugar, and vanilla in a medium-size heavy saucepan to blend, and bring to a boil over medium heat. Add the chocolate and whisk until all the chocolate has melted. Remove from the heat.

Using a whisk, stir the egg yolks in a large bowl to blend. Then, in a slow, steady stream, add the chocolate-cream mixture, whisking until smooth. Divide the mixture among 6 ramekins or small custard cups (each about 5½ ounces), and place them in a large high-sided baking dish or roasting pan. Carefully transfer the pan to the center rack in the oven. Add enough cold water to the baking dish so that it comes halfway up the sides of the ramekins. Bake for about 1 hour, or until the custards jiggle slightly in the center when gently shaken (the custards will thicken as they chill). Let cool to room temperature, and then refrigerate until cold.

chocolate soufflés

A great chocolate soufflé is something that can't be beat: light and yet really fulfilling. Some chocolate soufflés are made simply with cocoa, but this recipe has chocolate and cocoa, and the result is to die for. If you're feeling really indulgent, break open the tops of the soufflés and pour some heavy cream into them.

Serves 6

1 tablespoon (⅛ stick) unsalted butter

⅓ cup sugar, plus more for coating soufflé dishes

4 ounces good-quality dark chocolate (60% to 70% cacao), coarsely chopped

½ cup cold water

⅓ cup unsweetened cocoa powder

6 large egg whites

Confectioners' sugar

Preheat the oven to 350°F. Coat the interiors of six 7.75-ounce soufflé dishes completely with the butter; then coat them with sugar. Place the dishes on a baking sheet.

Stir the chopped chocolate in a large bowl set over a saucepan of simmering water until it is melted and smooth. Whisk in the cold water and the cocoa powder. Remove from the heat and set aside.

Using an electric mixer fitted with the whisk attachment, beat the egg whites in a large bowl until they are foamy. Gradually beat in the ⅓ cup sugar. Continue beating until the egg whites are shiny and form soft peaks when the whisk is removed. Fold a fourth of the egg white mixture into the warm chocolate mixture. Fold in the remaining egg white mixture (the new mixture will resemble chocolate mousse). Divide the soufflé batter equally among the prepared soufflé dishes.

Bake the soufflés until they puff but are still moist in the center, about 12 minutes. Lightly dust with confectioners' sugar and serve immediately.

tiramisù

Tiramisù lives and dies by the amount of espresso it contains. If you don't soak the ladyfingers enough, the dessert will be dry; if they are too sodden, they will disintegrate before you can assemble the dish. I use a pastry brush to give the cookies an extra hit of espresso, so when you break through the custard with your spoon you get a creamy molten bite of espresso, not dry cookie.

Serves 6

2/3 cup strong brewed espresso

1/2 cup brandy

4 large egg yolks

4 tablespoons sugar

2 cups mascarpone cheese, at room temperature

2 large egg whites

About 30 crisp Italian ladyfinger cookies (Savoiardi)

Bittersweet chocolate, for grating

Combine the cold espresso and brandy in a small bowl.

Fill a saucepan halfway with water and bring to a simmer. Set a shallow metal bowl on top of the saucepan. Using a handheld electric mixer, beat the egg yolks and 2 table-spoons of the sugar in the metal bowl until the mixture is pale and thick and forms a ribbon when the beaters are lifted, about 4 minutes. Remove the bowl from the heat and let it cool for 5 minutes.

Place the mascarpone in a large bowl. Stir half of the egg yolk mixture into the mascarpone to lighten it; then fold in the remaining yolk mixture.

In another large bowl and using clean beaters, beat the egg whites and the remaining 2 tablespoons sugar with the electric mixer just until stiff peaks form. (The beaters must be clean and dry in order for the egg whites to beat up to their full volume.) Fold the egg whites into the mascarpone mixture.

Spoon a thin layer of the mascarpone mixture over the bottom of a 1 1/2-quart trifle bowl. Using enough cookies to form a layer over the mascarpone mixture, quickly submerge the cookies in the espresso-brandy mixture and then remove them, allowing any excess liquid to drip back into the bowl. Arrange the cookies in a single layer over the mascarpone mixture. With a pastry brush, brush some additional espresso-brandy mixture onto the cookies for a more intense coffee flavor. Spread more mascarpone mixture over the cookies to form another layer. Repeat with the remaining cookies, espresso-brandy mixture, and mascarpone mixture to create layers, ending with the mascarpone mixture. Grate the cho-colate over the tiramisù. Refrigerate until set, about 2 hours.

brownie cupcakes

If you ever need to silence a room, serve a plate of these—they are so chewy and decadent. Imagine a cross between cupcakes and brownies, and you'll see why people go wild for them.

Makes 8

Cupcakes

6 ounces good-quality bittersweet chocolate (60% to 70% cacao), chopped

6 tablespoons (¾ stick) unsalted butter

1 tablespoon Lyle's Golden Syrup or light corn syrup

Pinch of salt

¾ cup sugar

2 large eggs

½ cup all-purpose flour

1 teaspoon baking powder

⅔ cup coarsely chopped walnuts

Frosting

4 ounces cream cheese, at room temperature

⅓ cup Lyle's Golden Syrup or light corn syrup

4 ounces good-quality bittersweet chocolate (60% to 70% cacao), chopped

8 small fresh strawberries

To make the cupcakes: Position an oven rack in the center of the oven and preheat the oven to 350°F. Line a standard cupcake tin with 8 paper cupcake liners. Stir the chocolate and butter in a small heavy saucepan over low heat until they melt and the mixture is smooth. Stir in the syrup and salt. Remove from the heat and set aside.

Using an electric mixer, beat the sugar and eggs in a large bowl for 2 minutes or until the mixture is thick and light. Stir in the chocolate mixture. Add the flour and baking powder, and stir just until blended; then stir in the walnuts. Divide the batter equally among the cupcake liners, filling them completely. Bake for about 25 minutes, or until the cupcakes puff and crack on top and a skewer inserted into the center of one comes out with fudgy crumbs attached. Remove the cupcakes from the tin and let them cool completely on a wire rack.

To frost the cupcakes: Using an electric mixer, beat the cream cheese in a large bowl until it is light and smooth. Beat in the syrup. Place the chocolate in another bowl and set the bowl over a small pot of simmering water. Stir constantly until the chocolate melts. Add the melted chocolate to the cream cheese mixture and beat until blended and fluffy, stopping the machine and scraping the bottom of the bowl to ensure that the mixture is well blended. Spread the frosting generously over the cooled cupcakes. Garnish each one with a fresh strawberry, and serve.

peanut butter cookies with chocolate chunks

To me, America is the home of good cookies—you can get so many great ones here. I was telling my fabulous food editor, Rochelle, how much I love the fresh-baked ones you get in-flight on certain airlines, and said that I hadn't managed to make any that were as good, and we came up with this recipe together. They are outstanding at any altitude.

Makes about 20 cookies

1 cup all-purpose flour

½ teaspoon baking soda

½ teaspoon salt

1 cup natural chunky peanut butter (about 9 ounces)

½ cup (packed) light brown sugar

½ cup granulated sugar

8 tablespoons (1 stick) unsalted butter, at room temperature

2 tablespoons honey

1 large egg

1 teaspoon pure vanilla extract

5 ounces semisweet chocolate, coarsely chopped

Preheat the oven to 350°F. Line 3 large heavy baking sheets with parchment paper.

Mix the flour, baking soda, and salt in a medium bowl. Using an electric mixer, beat the peanut butter, brown sugar, granulated sugar, butter, honey, egg, and vanilla in a large bowl until well blended. Stir the dry ingredients into the peanut butter mixture in two additions. Stir in the chopped chocolate.

Scoop about 3 tablespoonsful of dough for each cookie onto the prepared baking sheets, spacing them 2½ inches apart. Bake for about 12 minutes, or until the cookies puff and begin to brown on top but are still very soft to the touch. Let the cookies cool on the baking sheets for 5 minutes. Then use a metal spatula to transfer the cookies to a wire rack. Enjoy the cookies warm or let them cool completely.

amaretto hot chocolate floats with vanilla swiss almond ice cream

There is something so warm and comforting about hot chocolate—but I couldn't resist gilding the lily with a scoop of ice cream. Each bite has a contrast of temperatures and textures, and you'll find it so entertaining to eat: It's a race against time to consume this before the ice cream has completely melted into the molten chocolate.

Serves 4

1⅓ cups whole milk

⅓ cup amaretto or other almond-flavored liqueur

2 tablespoons sugar

4 ounces dark chocolate (bittersweet or semisweet), chopped

¾ cup heavy cream

1 pint vanilla Swiss almond ice cream

Shaved chocolate, optional

Combine the milk, amaretto, and sugar in a medium saucepan and bring to a near simmer over medium heat, stirring until the sugar dissolves.

While the milk is heating, place the chopped chocolate in a metal bowl and set the bowl over the saucepan of milk, stirring until the chocolate is melted and smooth. Check every now and then to make sure the milk is not simmering. Whisk the melted chocolate into the hot milk mixture, and keep warm.

Beat the heavy cream in a large bowl until soft peaks form. Place a scoop of ice cream in each of 4 bowls. Pour the hot chocolate mixture over the ice cream, and top with the whipped cream and shaved chocolate, if using. Serve immediately.

blueberry clafoutis

Clafoutis are the perfect light ending to a heavy meal. Because they are so soft and delicate, they are best made in single servings so they look as pretty in front of your guests as they do when they come out of the oven. Serve this custardy dessert while it is still warm. I overload the clafoutis with berries so that they are seriously moist.

Serves 6

Clafoutis

¾ cup sliced almonds

⅔ cup granulated sugar

1 tablespoon all-purpose flour

½ teaspoon salt

2 large eggs

3 large egg yolks

1¼ cups heavy cream

About 1 tablespoon unsalted butter

¾ cup fresh blueberries

Blueberry cream

1 cup heavy cream

1 cup fresh blueberries

For dusting

Confectioners' sugar

Preheat the oven to 400°F.

Spread the almonds on a baking sheet and toast until golden, 7 to 8 minutes, stirring once or twice. Transfer to a food processor and let cool for a few minutes. Add the granulated sugar, flour, and salt to the food processor and blend until the almonds are very finely ground. Blend in the eggs and egg yolks. Add the cream and continue to blend until a smooth batter forms. Transfer the batter to a 4-cup measuring cup. Cover and refrigerate for 12 hours.

Butter the inner sides of six 4-inch-diameter tartlet pans. Arrange the pans on a large heavy baking sheet. Divide the blueberries among the prepared tartlet pans.

Stir the batter to blend, and then pour it over the blueberries. Bake the clafoutis for about 12 minutes, or until the filling rises slightly, is lightly set, and is beginning to brown on top. Cool for 5 minutes; then invert them onto a wire cooling rack and remove the tartlet pans.

To make the blueberry cream: In a large bowl, using a handheld electric mixer, whisk the cream and blueberries for 2 minutes or until the cream is semi-whipped. Set aside.

Transfer the clafoutis to plates, dust them with confectioners' sugar, and serve with the blueberry cream.

lemon curd tarts
with fresh raspberries

Lemon curd is one of the first things my mum taught me to make. We used to have it for breakfast on hot toast with a bit of butter—delicious! It's great in these easy tarts but also nice spooned over ice cream. The curd can be made up to a week ahead and refrigerated; the shells can be stored in an airtight container at room temperature for a day or two. Simply fill the shells with the curd before serving. This is a light dessert; you don't need to use too much lemon curd in each one. See the photograph on page 227.

Serves 4

Pastry shells

12 sheets filo dough (each about 17x12 inches)

About 8 tablespoons (1 stick) unsalted butter, melted

Filling

4 large eggs

1 cup sugar

$\frac{1}{2}$ cup fresh lemon juice

1 tablespoon grated lemon zest

8 tablespoons (1 stick) salted butter, diced

$1\frac{1}{2}$ cups fresh raspberries

Confectioners' sugar, for garnish

To make the pastry shells: Preheat the oven to 350°F. Place 1 sheet of filo pastry on a dry flat surface and brush it with some of the melted butter. Place another sheet of filo on top of the first sheet, and brush it with more melted butter. Repeat this process until 6 sheets of the filo are stacked on top of each other. Cut the stack of filo sheets into two 7-inch squares; discard the trimmings. Gently press each stack into a shallow $4\frac{1}{2}$-inch-diameter tartlet pan. Using kitchen shears, trim away the excess pastry, leaving about $\frac{1}{2}$ inch of pastry above the rims of the tart pans. Place the tart pans on a heavy baking sheet. Repeat with the remaining 6 filo sheets and melted butter. Bake the pastry shells for 15 to 20 minutes or until dark golden brown. Carefully lift the shells from the pans and place them on a wire rack to cool completely.

To make the filling: Bring a large saucepan of water to a boil over medium-high heat. Reduce the heat to low. Whisk the eggs, sugar, lemon juice, and lemon zest in a medium stainless steel or glass bowl to blend. Place the bowl over the hot water and whisk in the butter. Continue to whisk for about 3 minutes, or until the lemon curd has become thick and creamy and coats the back of a spoon. Remove the bowl from the heat and whisk until most of the heat has dissipated from the lemon curd, about 10 minutes. Set the lemon curd aside to cool completely; stir it occasionally while it is cooling. (The curd will continue to thicken as it cools.)

nectarine and raspberry sundae

I sometimes feel that certain ingredients are just meant to be served together, and raspberries and nectarines are just such a pairing. While this isn't exactly health food, it's certainly a lighter, healthier alternative to a chocolate sundae, and a tray of these brought out after an outdoor feast is a beautiful and fun way to end the meal.

Serves 6

3 half-pint baskets fresh raspberries

⅔ cup confectioners' sugar

4 ripe nectarines, pitted and cubed

1 quart nonfat all-natural vanilla frozen yogurt

Combine 2 baskets of the raspberries and the ⅔ cup confectioners' sugar in a blender or food processor, and process until smooth. Strain the raspberry puree through a fine-mesh sieve into a small bowl, pressing on the solids with a rubber spatula. Discard the solids. Set the sauce aside.

Layer the nectarines, frozen yogurt, and raspberry sauce in 6 glasses. Garnish with the remaining raspberries, and serve immediately.

plum and cinnamon crumble

The best part of a crisp, or its cousin the crumble, is the way the butter in the crumbly topping melts over the fruit to infuse it with flavor. I put a whole cinnamon stick in this filling to add another layer of flavor. Crumbles and crisps are really quick to put together, but they can also be assembled in advance and held in the refrigerator for a couple of hours until you are ready to bake them. Place the crumble in the oven ten minutes before you serve the main course so you can serve it warm.

Serves 6

Filling

2 pounds plums, halved, pitted, each cut into 6 wedges

⅓ cup sugar

2 cinnamon sticks

Topping

¾ cup all-purpose flour

½ cup sugar

½ cup rolled oats (not instant)

8 tablespoons (1 stick) cold unsalted butter, cut into pieces

¾ cup sliced almonds, coarsely chopped

Vanilla ice cream, for serving

Preheat the oven to 350°F. To make the filling: Toss the plums, sugar, and cinnamon sticks in an 8-inch-square baking dish. Arrange the mixture evenly in the dish, tucking the cinnamon sticks beneath the plums.

To make the topping: Mix the flour, sugar, and oats in a medium bowl to blend. Using your fingers, work the butter into the flour mixture until moist clumps form. Mix in the almonds. Sprinkle the crumb topping evenly over the plum mixture.

Bake for 45 minutes, or until the juices are bubbling, the fruit is tender, and the topping is golden brown. Allow the crumble to stand at room temperature for 5 minutes before serving.

Spoon the crumble into bowls, discarding the cinnamon sticks, and serve with vanilla ice cream.

grilled pineapple skewers with coconut and caramel sauce

When you are serving a grill menu, it's nice to end the evening with something equally casual so you can carry on the evening without a change of mood—or locale. The caramel sauce and coconut can be prepared the day before, making the whole thing hassle-free. Canned coconut milk has a rich, thick layer of cream that floats on top of the coconut milk, so don't shake the can before you open it; use as much of that cream as possible to make the caramel sauce.

Serves 4

Coconut caramel sauce

1/2 cup sugar

1 cup unsweetened heavy coconut milk (see headnote)

Pineapple skewers

2/3 cup sweetened shredded coconut

1 pineapple, peeled, cored, and cut into twenty 1-inch cubes

1 tablespoon (1/8 stick) unsalted butter, melted

Soak 20 bamboo skewers in warm water for 30 minutes.

To make the coconut caramel sauce: Stir the sugar and 2 tablespoons water in a small heavy saucepan over medium heat for about 2 minutes, or until the sugar dissolves. Simmer the melted sugar without stirring, brushing down the sides of the pan with a wet pastry brush to remove any sugar crystals and swirling the pan occasionally, for about 8 minutes, or until it becomes golden brown. Immediately add the coconut milk and stir to blend (the mixture will bubble vigorously when the milk is added). Simmer over medium heat for about 3 minutes, or until the caramel melts and the sauce thickens slightly. Remove the sauce from the heat and pour it into a serving bowl.

To prepare the pineapple skewers: Preheat the broiler to low heat. Sprinkle the coconut evenly over a baking sheet. Broil the coconut, stirring it occasionally, for 2 minutes or until it is lightly golden. (Watch the coconut closely while it broils to ensure it does not burn—it will color quite quickly.) Transfer the toasted coconut to a plate.

Remove the skewers from the water and thread 5 to 6 pieces of pineapple on each skewer.

Prepare a barbecue grill for medium-high heat. Brush the grill with the melted butter, and grill the pineapple cubes for 1 to 2 minutes on each side, or until they are heated through and grill marks appear. Remove the pineapple skewers from the grill or pan, and place them on a serving platter. Drizzle with caramel and sprinkle with coconut.

caramelized baby bananas
with almond brittle

These baby bananas could not be simpler. You leave them in the skin for cooking and serving, which makes them not only easier to cook but also easier to serve. Use shards of the brittle to scrape the banana out of its skin for a sugary, nutty taste with each bite.

Serves 4

2 cups whole almonds

2 cups granulated sugar

$\frac{1}{2}$ cup (packed) light brown sugar

6 baby bananas, cut in half lengthwise (peels left on)

Preheat the oven to 350°F. Place the almonds on a heavy baking sheet and bake, stirring occasionally to ensure that they brown evenly, for about 10 minutes, or until they are pale golden and fragrant. Set them aside to cool.

Line a baking sheet with parchment paper. Combine the granulated sugar and $\frac{1}{4}$ cup water in a medium-size heavy saucepan. Stir over medium heat until the sugar dissolves. Raise the heat and boil without stirring, occasionally swirling the pan and brushing down the sides with a pastry brush dipped in water, until the caramel is a deep amber color, about 8 minutes. Add the almonds and stir to coat them with the caramel. Quickly pour the almond mixture onto the prepared baking sheet and spread it out in an even layer. Allow the brittle to cool. Then break it into pieces.

Place the brown sugar on a plate. Using a small sharp knife, score the flesh side of the bananas. Press the bananas, flesh side down, in the brown sugar to coat them thickly. Heat a large nonstick frying pan over medium-high heat. Place the bananas, sugared side down, in the pan and cook for 2 minutes, or until the sugar has caramelized.

Transfer the caramelized bananas to plates, and serve with the almond brittle.

apple and pear upside-down
caramel tarts

The first time I tasted a tarte Tatin, I wondered why I had been wasting my time with any other dessert. Serve these after something light because they're just so good, your guests will be disappointed if they have a full stomach. These can also be done as large tarts if you have a group coming around. Simply roll out two pastry sheets into 8-inch squares and trim the corners to form rounds, and use two 8-inch cake pans to bake the tarts.

Serves 4

Caramel sauce

1½ cups sugar

8 tablespoons (1 stick) unsalted butter, at room temperature

½ teaspoon ground cinnamon

½ cup heavy cream

Tarts

2 Granny Smith apples, peeled, quartered, cored, and cut into ½-inch-thick wedges

2 Anjou pears, peeled, quartered, cored, and cut into ½-inch-thick wedges

1 sheet frozen puff pastry, thawed

To make the caramel sauce: Stir the sugar and ⅓ cup water in a medium-size heavy saucepan over medium heat, occasionally brushing down the sides of the pan with a wet pastry brush to remove any sugar that clings to the sides, until the sugar dissolves and the syrup comes to a simmer. (The sugar that clings to the side of the pan has a tendency to crystallize and ruin the silky consistency of the caramel, so wiping the sugar off the sides of the pan will help prevent this from happening.) Allow the sugar syrup to boil without stirring, for about 8 minutes or until it begins to turn golden brown. You will need to watch the syrup closely, as it can burn quite easily. Remove the pan from the heat. Add the butter and whisk until the butter melts and the mixture is smooth. Stir in the cinnamon.

Pour three fourths of the caramel sauce into four 4-inch-diameter cake pans with at least 1¾-inch-high sides, dividing it equally. Allow the caramel to cool in the pans. Whisk the cream into the remaining caramel sauce to blend, and set it aside.

To make the tarts: Arrange a layer of the apples and pears decoratively over the caramel in the pans; then stack the remaining apples and pears to fill the pans completely.

Unfold the pastry on a work surface and press the seams together if necessary. Cut out four 4-inch rounds. Place the

pastry rounds over the apples and pears, and tuck the pastry down into the sides of the pans. Prick the pastry 5 or 6 times with a fork or a small sharp knife. Cover the tarts with plastic wrap and refrigerate them for at least 1 hour and up to 1 day to chill the pastry.

Preheat the oven to 450°F. Transfer the tarts to a baking sheet and bake for about 30 minutes, or until the pastry is golden brown and cooked

through and the apples are very tender. Let the tarts rest at room temperature for 20 minutes to allow the flavors to meld and the juices to cool and thicken slightly.

Invert a plate over each tart. In a swift movement, invert each tart onto each plate. Remove the cake pans. Drizzle some of the reserved caramel sauce around the tarts, and serve. (Reserve any remaining caramel sauce in the refrigerator for another use.)

banoffee pie

This is the ultimate hybrid: a combination of banana and toffee in one incredible pie.

Serves 8

Crust

9 ounces graham crackers

8 tablespoons (1 stick) butter, melted

Toffee sauce

$1/2$ cup (packed) dark brown sugar

One 14-ounce can sweetened condensed milk

8 tablespoons (1 stick) butter

Filling

$1\frac{1}{4}$ cups heavy cream

5 small ripe bananas (about $1\frac{1}{2}$ pounds total)

To make the crust: Line the bottom of a 9-inch springform pan with parchment paper. Chop the graham crackers in a food processor until they are finely ground. Pour the melted butter over the crumbs and process to blend well. The crumbs should stick together when pressed. Press the crumb mixture over the bottom and $1\frac{1}{2}$ inches up the sides of the springform pan. Refrigerate.

To make the toffee sauce: Combine the brown sugar and 3 tablespoons water in a medium-size heavy saucepan. Stir over medium heat until the sugar dissolves. Raise the heat and boil without stirring, occasionally swirling the pan and brushing down the sides with a pastry brush dipped into water, until the syrup is a deep amber color, about 5 minutes. Stir in the condensed milk and butter. Continue stirring for 5 minutes or until the sauce thickens slightly.

Remove the toffee sauce from the heat, and spread 1 cup of the sauce over the prepared crust. Refrigerate for about 1 hour or until the toffee is semi-firm. Keep the remaining toffee sauce at room temperature.

To fill the pie: Using an electric mixer, beat the cream in a large bowl until thick and very soft billowy peaks form. Slice 3 of the bananas into very thin disks. Fold the sliced bananas into the softly whipped cream, and spoon the filling into the prepared pie crust.

Slice the remaining 2 bananas, and arrange the slices decoratively over the pie. Rewarm the remaining toffee sauce gently over low heat. Drizzle some of the sauce decoratively over the pie. (If the sauce has thickened too much to drizzle, stir a few tablespoons of milk into it.) Cut the pie into wedges, and transfer them to plates. Drizzle each pie wedge with more sauce, and serve.

individual strawberry cheesecakes
with aged balsamic vinegar

Strawberries and cheesecake work brilliantly together, and strawberries with balsamic vinegar is a classic Italian pairing. All three are even better together. The older balsamic gets, the sweeter it becomes; and used sparingly, it really is the perfect match for the creamy cheese. The biscotti add a bit more depth of flavor to the crust than would the usual graham crackers.

Serves 4

Crust

5$\frac{1}{2}$ ounces store-bought almond biscotti

4 tablespoons ($\frac{1}{2}$ stick) unsalted butter, melted

Filling

Two 8-ounce packages cream cheese, at room temperature

1 cup whole-milk cottage cheese, drained

$\frac{1}{2}$ cup sweetened condensed milk

$\frac{1}{4}$ cup sugar

1 large egg yolk

1$\frac{1}{2}$ teaspoons unflavored gelatin

8 fresh strawberries, hulled and finely diced

Topping

$\frac{1}{4}$ cup sugar

1 tablespoon fresh lemon juice

12 ounces fresh strawberries, hulled and quartered

2 teaspoons 10- to 20-year-old balsamic vinegar

To prepare the crust: Preheat the oven to 350°F. Line the bottoms and sides of four 4-inch-diameter springform pans (each pan should hold 1$\frac{1}{4}$ cups) with parchment paper. Finely grind the biscotti in a food processor. Blend the melted butter into the biscotti crumbs to form a moist, sandy texture. Press the crumb mixture evenly over the bottoms (not the sides) of the prepared pans. Place the pans on a baking sheet and bake the crusts for 18 minutes, or until they are pale golden brown. Allow them to cool completely in the pans.

To prepare the filling: Blend the cream cheese in a food processor until it is smooth and creamy, scraping down the sides and bottom of the bowl occasionally to ensure that no lumps remain. Add the cottage cheese and continue to blend until smooth and creamy. Add the sweetened condensed milk, sugar, and egg yolk and blend well. Leave the mixture in the processor.

Place $\frac{1}{4}$ cup water in a small saucepan. Sprinkle the gelatin over the water and let stand for 5 minutes or until the gelatin softens. Stir the gelatin mixture over medium heat for about 1$\frac{1}{2}$ minutes or until the gelatin dissolves. With the food processor running, slowly pour the hot gelatin mixture through the feed tube and into the cream cheese mixture in a thin stream. Continue to process to ensure that the gelatin is very well blended. Transfer the cream cheese mixture to a bowl and stir in the diced strawberries. Spoon the mixture into the cooled crust-lined pans, dividing it equally. Refrigerate for at least 3 hours, or until the cheesecakes are cold and set.

Remove the pan sides from the cheesecakes. Remove the cheesecakes from the pan bottoms and discard the parchment. Transfer them to individual serving plates. Use a small knife to smooth the sides of the cheesecakes, if necessary.

To prepare the topping: Combine ⅓ cup water, the sugar, and the lemon juice in a medium saucepan over medium heat, and simmer gently for 2 minutes, or until the sugar is dissolved and the mixture is syrupy. Add the strawberries and remove from the heat. Gently stir the mixture; the strawberries will soften slightly and flavor the syrup as it cools. Spoon the strawberry mixture over and around the individual cheesecakes. Drizzle ½ teaspoon of the balsamic vinegar over each cheesecake, and serve.

green tea ice cream

This is the real deal: a pure ice cream made with green tea and no artificial colors or flavors. It won't be the vivid green you may be used to—the color is a pale brownish green. Don't worry, though—the flavor provides the vibrance, and your guests will appreciate knowing that there are only pure, natural ingredients in their dessert.

Makes about 1½ quarts

2 cups heavy cream

2 cups whole milk

¼ cup green tea leaves

9 large egg yolks

1 cup sugar

Combine the cream and milk in a medium-size heavy saucepan and bring to a gentle simmer over medium heat. Add the tea leaves, remove from the heat, cover the pan, and let steep for 15 minutes.

Whisk the egg yolks and sugar in a large bowl for about 2 minutes, or until thick and creamy. Gradually whisk the tea mixture into the egg mixture to blend. Line a fine-mesh sieve with a paper towel, and strain the mixture into a clean saucepan.

Cook the custard over medium-low heat, stirring constantly, for 10 minutes, or until the custard coats the back of the spoon. Do not allow the custard to boil or it will curdle. Pour the custard into a large bowl and set the bowl into a larger bowl of ice water. Stir the custard until it is cold. Pour the custard into an ice-cream machine and process according to the manufacturer's instructions.

Scoop the ice cream into bowls, and serve.

rhubarb ripple ice cream

Since you're starting with a good-quality purchased ice cream, this is really easy to make. You can use any kind of fruit, but I grew up eating the rhubarb my mum grew in the backyard, and I love it. Its sharp flavor is a nice balance for ice cream, which can be a bit sweet for my taste. The rhubarb compote is simple to prepare—I always save some to have with my yogurt in the morning.

Makes about 1 quart

5 large stalks (1 pound) fresh rhubarb, coarsely chopped

¾ cup superfine sugar

2 tablespoons fresh lemon juice

1 vanilla bean, split lengthwise

1 quart good-quality vanilla ice cream

Ice-cream cones (optional)

Place the rhubarb, sugar, and lemon juice in a large heavy saucepan. Scrape in the seeds from the vanilla bean, and then add the bean itself. Cook over medium heat, stirring occasionally, for 25 minutes or until the rhubarb falls apart and the mixture is thick like a jam. Allow the compote to cool completely. Discard the vanilla bean.

Place the ice cream in a large mixing bowl and let it soften slightly (but not too much) in the refrigerator. Quickly stir the cooled rhubarb compote into the semi-softened ice cream, forming some swirls. Cover, and return to the freezer until firm.

Scoop the ice cream into bowls or ice-cream cones.

peach and honey cake
with orange syrup

This chewy cake is super-moist and so delicious that when you've made it once, I promise it will become a regular part of your repertoire. The syrup makes it very forgiving; even if you overbake it a touch, it won't seem dry.

Serves 8

Orange syrup

Grated zest and juice of
6 oranges

¼ cup sugar

½ vanilla bean, split lengthwise

Cake

¼ cup fresh lemon juice

3 tablespoons fresh lime juice

2 tablespoons orange blossom honey or other mild-flavored honey

1 tablespoon plus ¾ cup (1½ sticks) unsalted butter, at room temperature

1 pound ripe peaches (about 2 large), pitted, each cut into 8 wedges

¾ cup all-purpose flour

1 teaspoon baking powder

Pinch of salt

¾ cup sugar

2 tablespoons grated lemon zest

1 tablespoon grated lime zest

4 large eggs

Confectioners' sugar, for dusting

Heavy cream, for drizzling

To make the orange syrup: Combine the orange zest and juice, sugar, and vanilla bean in a small saucepan over medium-low heat and simmer for 8 minutes, or until the mixture is reduced and syrupy. Set the syrup aside to cool; discard vanilla bean.

To make the cake: Stir the lemon juice, lime juice, honey, and the 1 tablespoon butter in a large heavy saucepan over high heat for 5 minutes or until the mixture thickens. Add the peaches and cook for 2 minutes, or until they soften slightly and the juices thicken. Spoon the peach mixture onto a baking sheet and let it cool completely.

Preheat the oven to 350°F. Spray a 9-inch-diameter springform cake pan with nonstick cooking spray. Line the bottom of the pan with parchment paper. Whisk the flour, baking powder, and salt in a medium bowl to blend. Set it aside. Using an electric mixer, beat the remaining ¾ cup butter with the sugar, lemon zest, and lime zest in a large bowl until light and fluffy. Add the eggs, one at a time, beating well after each addition before adding the next. Add the flour mixture and mix just until blended. Transfer the batter to the prepared cake pan.

Arrange the peaches in a single layer atop the batter. Bake for 10 minutes. Then reduce the heat to 300°F and bake for 1 hour longer, or until the cake is golden brown on top and beginning to pull away from the sides of the pan. Transfer the cake pan to a wire rack and let it cool for 30 minutes.

Run a small sharp knife around the sides of the pan to loosen the cake. Remove the pan sides. Transfer the warm cake to a platter, and dust it with confectioners' sugar. Cut the cake into wedges, and transfer them to plates. Drizzle the orange syrup and the cream over each slice of warm cake, and serve.

acknowledgments

I feel like the luckiest man in the world. Not only do I get to work with my favorite thing in the world each day, food, I also get to work very closely with one of my favorite people. Jodie Gatt, you are extremely talented, completely charming to everyone you meet, and bloody great fun to have a glass of wine with. (I would also like to thank your boyfriend, Damien, for still talking to me when we are often kept working until the early hours of the morning.)

I have had the great pleasure of working with an incredible food editor, Rochelle Palermo, who would have to be the most thorough individual in the food industry today. Thanks for your amazing organization and meticulous recipe testing. Rochelle also managed to pull together a group of young chefs-in-the-making who came to every day of our shoot and helped me cook and style all the food you see. It's this kind of dedication that makes the food industry what it is, so a huge thanks to Kathryn Mirtsopoulos, Justin Hicks, Stephanie Romer, and Leigh Regan Baragona.

I was also lucky enough to work with an incredible food photographer whom I have admired for years. Quentin Bacon happens to be an Aussie living in New York, and as an added bonus, he let me cook in the studio while he conducted a casting full of beautiful models. Love your work, mate. Quentin recommended Pamela De Silver as a prop stylist, and she was simply wonderful.

My great editor, Pam Krauss, allowed me plenty of freedom and was there to help pick up the pieces when my introductions needed some work. Pam, thanks for getting the words out of my head and onto the page—you're the best! Subtitle has done a wonderful job with the design of the book; every time I look at a layout I feel relaxed. Finally, one last thank-you to Jay Mandel at the William Morris Agency for making it all possible.

index